The Butterfly Collector

Rick:
    Thanks for your
encouragement and support.

        Fred McYman

The
BUTTERFLY
COLLECTOR

stories

Fred
McGavran

Black Lawrence Press
New York

Black Lawrence Press
www.blacklawrence.com

Executive Editor and Art Director: Colleen Ryor
Managing Editor: Diane Goettel
Book Design: Steven Seighman

Black Lawrence Press
8405 Bay Parkway C8
Brooklyn, N.Y. 11214
U.S.A.

Published 2009 by Black Lawrence Press, an imprint of Dzanc Books

First edition 2009
ISBN: 978-0-9815899-3-0

Printed in the United States

This is a work of fiction. Any resemblance to actual persons, living or dead, or events is entirely coincidental.

CONTENTS

For Liz
Who is not Lillian

THE
BUTTERFLY
COLLECTOR

T he link between butterflies and dreams is poorly understood. I had accompanied my wife Lillian and her Mother to the butterfly exhibit at the conservatory more out of a sense of duty than any interest in butterflies or in them. After thirty-seven years of marriage, we spent Sunday afternoons seeking some diversion that Lillian and Mother's feet and nerves and bladders could endure. While they were distracted by the orchids, I slipped away on a concrete path through the imitation rain forest, steamy with drizzle from overhead pipes. We had been there so often that I recognized the overfed goldfish in the jungle pool and many of the family groups pretending to share grandma's interest in exotic flowers. *Just another three hours,* I thought, *and Lillian will think of dinner, I can open a bottle of wine, and the evening will merge with all the others in the soft gauze of forgetfulness and boredom.*

I don't remember entering the exhibit itself. High school girls in khaki shorts and bright green polo shirts were passing out a brochure called "How to Identify Butterflies," and children were staring at the trees. It was strangely quiet. According to the brochure, ants tended one family, the Lycaenids, until they emerged from their cocoons a beautiful silvery blue. Perhaps that's why they wobbled so unsteadily when they finally escaped; the sun came upon them too quickly.

Then a boy started to run, and a girl shouted, "You're not allowed to catch them!"

.I saw something flutter, and my chest froze. Brighter than strobe lights, more brilliant than fireworks, the butterflies flickered among the palms. Slivers of orange and silver and blue opened and closed like slits into eternity. I felt my way to a bench and sat down. Inside the silent bursts, saints and angels appeared and beckoned only to vanish when I focused on them.

Around me children held out their hands, and mothers said, "Be careful." Like aerial sprites, butterflies reeled through the foliage and hovered just above the grasping fingers. A silver butterfly wavered over me, opening the firmament to the reign of Elizabeth the First. The old lady trotted through the crowd on an enormous white horse. I reached out to touch her skirt.

"Where have you been?" Lillian demanded. "Mother's absolutely exhausted. I had to take her to the car."

Always before, this was Lillian's welcome signal to disengage. But who can move so abruptly from cheering the Queen's lancers to the long drive home with Mother?

"Can't we stay another few minutes?" I begged.

"No."

Like a mother with a recalcitrant five-year-old, she took my arm and led me to the gate. An old man in a pith helmet sat beside the screen door.

"Just one at a time," he cautioned. "We don't want any of our guests to escape."

"Mother is waiting," Lillian snapped, pushing me through the door into a screened enclosure. In the corner of my eye I saw something silver.

"Be careful!" the guardian cried. "He's getting away!"

Lillian kept going through the next door, and that gave me my chance. Like a naughty child, I reached out and cupped the butterfly in my hand. Looking back, I saw the old man wag his finger at me. When we reached the car, Mother was sitting in the front seat, fanning herself with the service leaflet from church.

"Where were you?" she greeted me.

"Banbury Cross," I replied.

"Don't be ridiculous," she snapped.

The butterfly tickled my hand. Lillian had to buckle my seat belt because I was holding the butterfly in one hand and the brochure in the other. In the evening, after she had driven Mother back to the retirement center, I would hear more about this exchange.

As we crept along the parkway, Lillian and Mother discussed the low quality of the cleaning service at the center. Cupping my hand like a telescope, I peered out the window to see what the butterfly was doing. Nothing. What had happened? Breathless, I started to open my fingers, and saw a blackness deeper than the blackness beyond the last galaxies. Then a tiny light appeared, rising from the depths of space and splitting and swirling until the Milky Way turned slowly in my hand. Who had ever seen this but God? If I opened my hand, our universe would dissolve; if I closed my fist, all creation would be crushed. It trembled in my hand, wanting so much to stay alive. I was weeping when Lillian opened the door to unfasten my seat belt and say that we were home.

I slipped into my study while Lillian and Mother fussed over who would use the bathroom first. Carefully opening my fingers, I watched the butterfly stretch its wings like a child yawning and rise effortlessly to the top of the bookshelf. Then I went to the kitchen to pour the sherry. I don't like sherry, but Lillian won't allow us anything stronger. Sometimes, on Sundays, she and Mother spread cream cheese on Ritz crackers as an hors d'oeuvre. They do not expect me to join them in conversation.

Dinner began uneventfully. Lillian had boiled something that my regular Chardonnay could not quite overcome. She and Mother were exchanging ideas about basting, when I saw it wavering over the highboy. The butterfly had slipped in from the den and was sitting at the edge of the scroll, where only I could see it. I raised my glass to it, as I once had to Lillian at the cotillion that last summer before our engagement.

"Did you say something, dear?" she asked.

"No."

The air was soft, the orchestra restrained, and the only name on my dance card was hers. Her hair smelled clean, and her eyes were soft and blue. How could I know that the decades would strain the life out of them, and her hands would turn hard and cold? But now we were young and the windows were open to the soft night, and none of this could ever happen to us.

"It's the wine," Mother said. "With all his medicines, you shouldn't let him drink like that."

I don't take that many medicines. Like everyone else, I'm on Lipitor and something for my blood pressure and allergies, and the doctor recently added Aricept as a stimulant. I was going to ask about dessert, but the butterfly had separated from the highboy and was struggling through the air conditioning to the living room. If I did anything to divert their attention from me, they might see it, and out would come the fly swatters and the Raid.

"He hasn't even asked about dessert," Lillian said.

I went to bed as soon as she left to drive Mother back to Bright Acres. When you have seen the Queen, the creation of the universe, and revisited your youth in an afternoon, you have a lot to think about before going to sleep. I was just closing my eyes, when I realized the butterfly had followed me to the bedroom and alighted on the ceiling light fixture. Then Santa Sophia was lit again with a thousand candles, and I was staring into the enormous eyes of Christos Pantocrator on the glittering dome. Darker than the second before creation, indifferent to prayer and incense, they stared through the terrified worshippers, until they started to turn to me.

"No!" I cried, holding my hands over my face. "Don't look at me!"

For if those eyes met mine, they would see my sins and pinion me in hell.

"What on earth is the matter?" Lillian said.

For the first time in thirty years, I was glad to hear her voice.

"You have to stop drinking so much wine," she scolded and went into the bathroom.

The mosaic disappeared beneath the Turkish conqueror's whitewash. Lillian flushed the toilet twice, then rattled the handle to stop it from running. When she finally came to bed, she pulled on the sheet and told me to stop talking to myself.

The next ten days, before Lillian took me to the doctor, were the happiest in my life. After breakfast the butterfly followed me when I took my coffee and the newspaper to the screen porch. Sometimes I could see the events of the day compressed between its wings; sometimes we would fly together to Florence, or Jerusalem, or the Islands of the Blest. By lunchtime I was ready for a glass of milk and my sandwich and nap. Then in the afternoons we would sit together smelling the rain through the screens and watch wooden ships lumber with the trade winds across blue-black seas. After dinner we retired to my study to see the lives of the saints emblazoned in a moving book of hours, or witness terrifying martyrdoms during the reign of Diocletian.

"He hasn't spoken for a week," Lillian said to Dr. Morris. "Mother and I are beside ourselves."

"The same thing happened to her father," Mother added to demonstrate her competence in geriatrics. "Do you think it's genetic?"

Dr. Morris was not interested in genetics. He was moving a finger in front of my eyes to see if I could follow it. I stared at his forehead; he wasn't wearing the round reflector doctors are supposed to wear to see your tonsils when you say "Aaaa". He didn't even have one of those wooden tongue depressors, twice as thick as Popsicle sticks that they stick down your throat until you gag.

"Aaaa," I said to see if he was a real doctor.

That was a mistake. The doctor leaned back and smiled professionally.

"Thank you, Walter," he said.

"You shouldn't be encouraging him, should you, doctor?" Lillian asked.

"Many times they remember things that happened when they were children, and forget what happened in the waiting room."

"I don't know how that nurse will ever forgive us," Mother said.

There was nothing to forgive. If she didn't want men stuffing bank notes in her garter, she should not be in the chorus at the Moulin Rouge.

"The worst times are when he is afraid," Lillian continued.

I knew where this was going: an institution, furtive consultations with bank officers, then Lillian and Mother would be off for a month on the QE 3 to regain their composure. Like Lear I had made many mistakes, and like Lear I would not go quietly.

"Where are you going?" Dr. Morris cried, but I was too quick for him.

Unlike Lear, however, I had no Fool to guide me. I got through the waiting room and into the corridor, but where should I go next? They caught me in the elevator staring at the buttons, unable to decide whether to go up or down to escape.

"I'm sure he'll be fine at home, until a bed opens up in the Alzheimer's unit," Dr. Morris said as we parted. "They're much more comfortable among familiar things."

"And no more alcohol," Mother added.

The nurse from the Moulin Rouge held my hand until I was safely belted in the car.

"Tonight, after the second show?" I whispered.

"Oh, no, they probably won't have anything for several days," she replied.

After so many years with Lillian and her Mother, I was used to people talking about me as if I didn't exist. The next two days, however, they didn't talk at all. I was blissfully happy. The butterfly and I sat together in the den; they wouldn't let me out on the porch anymore. Sometimes I just held it on my finger and watched its feelers tremble.

Other times it perched on the bookshelves and showed me mysteries that only angels can comprehend.

"If he doesn't eat something, he's going to make himself sick," Mother said.

"Would you like a nice turkey sandwich?" Lillian tempted me.

I did not reply. It's so hard to find the right wine for turkey and mayonnaise, and if we did, it would only lead to another argument. So much better to cup the butterfly in my fingers and find sustenance in its thoughts. After all, butterflies live on sugar water and sunshine.

"What's he holding?" Mother asked.

I closed my fist so they could not see it.

"Walter, what is that?" Lillian demanded.

"I'll bet it's his medicine," Mother said. "He hasn't been taking his medicine."

If only I hadn't been taking my medicine, my reflexes might have been better.

"Here," Lillian said, grabbing my hand. "Let me see."

Like an angry mother searching for chewing gum, she started to pry my fingers apart.

"Give it to me!"

Wings beating like the heart of a little animal, the butterfly quivered inside my hand. I tried to keep it closed, but Lillian pulled harder and harder until my fingers ached like the time I shinnied up the swing set and fell to the ground from exhaustion.

"No!" was the last word I ever spoke.

Its silver wings were streaked against my palm like mercury from a broken thermometer. In one last second, I saw the mosaics shattered by the hammers of the infidels and women fleeing from the ruined city. And then my world went blank.

I don't know how long I will stay here. At first

they said it was just until my medication was adjusted, or until Lillian returned, or until the doctor did some more tests. Don, my caretaker, helps me dress and go to the bathroom and brings food on cafeteria trays. Sometimes we go to crafts or to the community room for ice cream and balloons. My favorite time is computer time, when they let me write whatever I want.

"Would you like to share that with doctor?" Don always asks.

I shake my head and smile, so Don will not be hurt. At the end of the session, I delete every word.

Whom can I talk to, after witnessing creation? To whom can I confess, now that I have seen through the eyes of God?

So I made a vow of silence to the butterfly, but not out of devotion. Like some illicit intoxicant, it brought unimaginable joy, then died and left me alone. If Alzheimer's were only a disease of the memory, I could forget. Can anyone who visited Ravenna when Justinian's mosaics were new or saw Vienna besieged by Suleiman the Magnificent ever forget? We do not mutter to ourselves and shamble through the halls because we don't remember, but because we have seen too much. So I don't mind them keeping me here, where you can tell the staff by their white tennis shoes, and the inmates by their expressions of unimaginable loss.

THE
BEAUTICIAN

S ome people can only confide in their beautician. I
never talk after a session. That's why I get so many
calls from the big hotels when a last minute pimple
threatens a bride or one of the dais guests at a fundraiser.
So it wasn't any surprise when the hospital called and
asked me to make up a patient in intensive care, although
I'd never heard the name before.

"Cookie, that's just weird," my Mother said when
I told her about my hospital clients.

I don't even argue with her about it anymore. Dying
people are very conscious of their appearance. I have sometimes
been with them at the end and sometimes afterwards. For
many of my clients, the pain on their faces is not from their
passing but at how they will look at the visitation. If a woman
has taken care of herself, closed casket is just not an option.

"I'm Cookie from the Gloria Feinman Salon," I said to the girl at the nursing station. "For Marion Devorest."

I always try to be pleasant. When they see somebody new coming down the hall with a makeup case, they might think you're a specialist with some weird therapy.

"Is anything special going on with her today?" I asked.

"It's Room 3321," she replied.

I used to leave my card at the desk, but I never got any new clients that way. Nurses never care much about their appearance.

"Thank you," I said.

She had that look like she wanted to tell somebody something, but it wasn't me.

A man in hospital greens was coming out of the room.

"I'm the beautician," I said. "For Marion."

"All ready for you," he said. "And you don't have to worry. It's nothing contagious."

It's nice when they say things to put you at ease.

"Thank you, Doctor," I smiled at him.

"Oh, no, I'm not the doctor," he said quickly. "I'm the nurse."

He held the door. Little things count with me. You never know whom you might meet on a job. When you're over thirty, you have to look around.

It was a private room, so dark I could barely see the patient under the twisted sheets. The side of the bed toward me was crowded with machines and hanging tubes.

"Can I help with anything?" the nurse asked from the door.

"Sometimes they have a picture I can use," I replied.

"Over here, dear," the patient said.

If trees could talk, they would whisper to each other in voices like that. It happens a lot to people who smoked unfiltered cigarettes in the 40s and 50s. I went around the bed away from the door. The tubes beside her rustled; she was trying to point with her IV hand. Pictures in old frames were neatly arranged on the bedside table. I found an empty space for my make up bag and drew up the guest chair. The door clicked shut as I sat down.

"You're so beautiful," I said, looking at the bride beside the man in uniform in a black and white photograph.

I always say something nice to make them feel comfortable with me.

"And here you are with the children."

A woman in an Esther Williams swimsuit stretched her long tan legs beside a pool, while two little boys and a girl splashed happily in the water behind her.

"Is it all right to call you Marion, Mrs. Devorest?" I asked.

"You're so sweet."

"Maybe we can use this," I said, picking up a portrait of the woman in her late forties, maybe about the time the children were going to college or being married, and she was spending more time on herself. Her hair was perfectly permed, and her complexion was smoother than any airbrush could make it.

"Can you make me look like that?" the voice asked anxiously.

"Let's see," I said, opening my kit.

Numbers flickered on the display panels on the other side of the bed. Their pale green light accented her wrinkles, making them dark as crevices on a ruined planet.

"Is it all right to turn on some light?

"Oh, no," the patient said quickly. "It's my eyes."

"Then let's start with your hair."

It was thin and broken and glued to her scalp with dried sweat. She started to cry.

"You don't know how awful it is to be like this," she sobbed.

"Let's just see what we can do."

I always try to be positive. It works pretty well with everybody except men.

I found a bowl in the bathroom and filled it with hot water. When I returned to the bed, she was still crying.

"There, there," I said, opening my makeup case and taking out my best aloe shampoo.

"I was afraid you had gone," she whispered. "I'm so old and ugly."

"Gone? Of course not. You'll be yourself again in just a few minutes."

She was wearing one of those awful hospital gowns that don't close in the back. When I sponged the hot water on her hair, she shuddered. The body under the sheet was breastless and angular, as if illness had stripped it of all femininity. She clutched the sheet to her chest. Then I started to rub in the shampoo, and she relaxed. It was as if her whole body was softening under the sheets, and even death waiting inside her was soothed.

She must have been sick for a long time; whoever had cut her hair had just chopped it off, leaving it ragged and spiky, with a little fluff to comb at the front. I took out my scissors to even it up. She wouldn't have a wave like the woman in the photograph, but nobody criticizes Ann Heche for her hair.

"Shall we put in a little color?" I asked.

"I've never used color," she said.

"Let's try," I said. "Then something to bring out the body. And you can call me Cookie."

Estelle Getty was beautiful when she died, because she paid attention to her hair. I used a little mousse, so she wouldn't lose the look so fast.

"Would you like to see?" I asked.

"I want to wait," she said. "Until everything's finished."

A lot of people are so afraid it won't work that they're afraid to look. I guess they want to keep on hoping. I took the bowl to the bathroom and filled it with fresh water for her face.

"Oh, oh," I said.

There were long strands of hair on her cheeks and chin, and her ears and nostrils were fuzzy. She must have come from one of those awful assisted living places, where all they do is change their diapers and feed them grilled cheese and juice. I had never seen eyebrows that long.

"Is something wrong?"

"No, dear," I said. "Everybody a certain age has the same problem."

That's why I carry a little razor and some shaving cream. If you do it just right, they never even know that you're shaving them. Then I tilted back her head and did her nostrils and ears and eyebrows with my cuticle scissors. I didn't dare try to pluck them. They looked like they'd been growing forever.

I rinsed off her face and patted it dry.

As I took out my foundation, I looked at the photograph of the woman with the permed hair and the perfect complexion. If she had not told me who was in the picture, I would never have thought it was Marion.

"Here," I said. "Let's try this."

I use foundation with moisturizer; her skin seemed to drink it in. I have never used so much on one person. As I smoothed it over her face, she leaned into my fingers like I was her husband touching her again after all these years.

"You're going to be just beautiful," I said.

She shuddered. I tell them all that, because they want so much to believe it. You have to be very careful with the powder and the blush with old people, so they don't look stained. And it's even harder without the right light. I use soft tones, so if someone were to turn up the lights, like for a code blue, she wouldn't look like she had already died.

When I started to put on the eye shadow, she took a quick breath.

"Am I hurting you, dear?" I asked.

A black blood vessel curled around the pupil of her right eye.

"What are you doing?"

"Making your eyes beautiful again."

"I didn't know things were so complicated for you girls, Cookie."

I smoothed on the eyeliner, then the mascara. She just dissolved.

"I've never felt anything so wonderful."

I took the bowl back to the bathroom and washed my hands.

"Are you ready to look now?" I asked.

"Yes."

So I took out my mirror, and the woman in the photograph, thirty years older, looked into the glass, just as she would before going out to a party. I have never seen such wonder and surprise. She started to cry again.

"Oh, no, don't do that," I said, patting her eyes with a tissue. "We'll have to do it all over again."

"I never imagined I could ever be like this."

I pressed her hand. So many are like that at the end. Her hand was gnarled like an old piece of wood, and her nails were broken stubs.

"Let me do your nails!" I exclaimed. "Do you like acrylics?"

"I've never used them."

"Then let's try," I said, taking out my acrylics and glue.

She watched while I shaped and glued a shiny new nail on each twisted finger.

"Now let's have some fun," I said. "How about bright red?"

"Do you really think so, Cookie?"

"Let's just see."

In ten minutes, her nails looked like she was fifty again.

"Do you want to go someplace to celebrate?" I asked, looking around for a walker. Sometimes they like to show off when it's finished. I'd noticed a family room down the corridor, where you could buy soft drinks and watch TV.

Just then somebody knocked at the door, and the nurse looked in.

"Father Spears is here, Marion," he said.

A man in his early sixties in a gray herringbone tweed jacket and clerical collar came in carrying a small case. For a crazy minute I thought he was going to make her up, too.

"Marion, how are you?" he asked before he was close enough to see.

Then he stopped and just stared at her, as if he couldn't think of the right words.

"You're beautiful," he finally said.

"Thank you so much, Charles."

She glowed in the light from the monitors. I finally understood why she had wanted me to make her up. From the way he was looking at her, they must have known each other a long time. His expression reminded me of someone. I glanced at the pictures on the table.

"I'm Charles Spears," he said, turning to me. "From the Downtown Church of Our Savior."

"I'm Cookie," I said. "From the Gloria Feinman Salon."

"Cookie, you're a genius," he said, taking my hand. "Marion's a different person."

He glanced at the table where I had spread out my things.

"I'm finished," I said, standing up.

"Oh, no," the priest said. "You can stay. I just need a little space."

Marion reached out and took my hand with her beautiful red nails so he could see them, too. I sat down and scooted the chair closer to the bed to give him more room. While he chatted with Marion about people at their church, he took out a silver cup and plate and a funny little bottle, and set them on a white cloth on the table. Then he opened a silver container and took out a little wafer and put it on the plate

"Would you like to participate in the Eucharist, Cookie?" he asked me.

"I'm Jewish," I said.

Mother always said not to leave them any doubt about that.

"Why don't you just sit there and hold Marion's hand," he said, taking the little bottle and pouring wine into the silver cup.

So I held her hand and sat there, and he took out a black book and started to read prayers. Marion knew some of them and said them along with him. Several times his voice started to break. I wondered what there had been between them. She was a lot older, but you can never tell.

Then he held up the wafer, broke it, and said it was the body of Christ, which I didn't understand at all, ate part of it and gave the rest to Marion. She released my hand and took it in her bright red nails while he took a sip of the wine. This time he held the cup out to her and said it was the blood of Christ. She dipped the wafer into the wine and ate it.

As he was saying another prayer, her hand started to tremble. I took it again, and she relaxed. Then he was packing up his case and ready to go, too. Marion lay back on her pillow, smiling like one of those women at a spa, who can just sleep the afternoon away. She was so happy I didn't want to let her go.

"I think Marion's asleep," the priest said.

I moved my fingers, and her hand dropped to the side of the bed. I stood up and packed up my things. When I moved away from the bed, the priest lifted Marion's hand and placed it on her chest. He made the sign of the cross on her forehead and hesitated, as if he wanted to do something that wasn't part of the ritual. Very slowly he bent over and kissed her forehead.

"Goodbye, Marion," he whispered.

The nurse knocked on the door and came in.

"Time to change your drip, Mr. Devorest," he said.

"We were just going," the priest said.

"Did you hear what he said?" I asked him when we were back in the hall. "'Mister' Devorest?"

"Oh," he said, surprised. "You didn't know."

For a minute I felt like I had to sit down.

"Marion was our senior warden when I first came to the church twenty-five years ago," he continued. "Showed me all the ropes. He was like a mother to me."

Father Spears had a nice way of talking to keep you from breaking up.

"He was a trust officer at one of the banks. He never married."

"What about those pictures?" I wondered.

This time he looked like the one who had to sit down.

"I loaned them to him when he went into assisted living, so he wouldn't look so alone. Even people who don't have family need someone around while they die."

People in hospital greens slid by us, as sleek and sexless as fish in a shallow sea.

"So who are they?"

"Those are my parents and me and my sister, when we were little," he said, his voice breaking again. "He had always admired them in my study. Especially my mother."

"That was your mother," I exclaimed.

"That was my mother."

We stopped beside the elevator. I must have looked awful.

"I feel like I've been used," I said bitterly.

He touched my arm.

"My mother died while I was away in seminary, Cookie. I never got to say goodbye."

"Oh, God," I whispered.

The elevator rang softly, and a family group wheeled out an old man with an IV drip hanging from a rod on his wheelchair.

"I have someone else to see down the corridor," the priest said.

"I only had the one appointment."

So I shook his hand and said goodbye. I wonder if we will ever work together again. Several days later, I saw Marion Devorest's obituary in the paper.

I have tried to find out, very discretely, whether anyone at the salon ever had a client like that. Enough beauticians have made up men, but you always know what's going on with those kind. I didn't figure it out about Mr. Devorest until it was finished. So I won't even tell my Mother. What we cover up is so much more important than what other people see.

TWO CURES FOR PHANTOM LIMB

After an amputation, the Doctor enjoyed a good cigar. Feet up on the couch, arms folded across his chest, he felt the tension, the screams, even the applause blend with the tobacco in a rich mixture that relaxed his body, stimulated his mind, and deadened his nostrils to the smell of blood.

The operation had been a success. The patient had lived, and the summer stars were shining brightly over the big house on the avenue. Through half-closed eyes, he watched the blue smoke drift over his red plush operating table and out the window into the garden, where his fourteen-year old son was burying the Brakeman's leg.

Frank, the Doctor's eldest son, enjoyed cigars and amputations, too. While his envious friends watched over the side fence, he set the lantern on the ground and dug as near to his mother's roses as he dared. His father had been a railroad doctor for ten years, and the yard was nearly full. When the hole was deep enough, Frank bowed to his friends and hurried into the house for the leg. With any luck, his father would leave his half-smoked cigar in the ashtray beside the couch and attribute its absence the next morning to an overly fastidious wife.

"Keep it wrapped in that sheet," the Doctor cautioned as his son entered the dark operating room. "A man's leg is entitled to some respect."

"Yes, Sir," Frank said.

He lifted the porcelain bowl from the stand beside the operating table. Unbalanced, the leg swung out and the toes touched the floor, as if they knew their fate and were trying to run away. Frank set down the bowl and picked up the leg with both hands.

Outside, he looked carefully at the house to be sure his father was not watching. The window was dark. He waved to his audience for silence. Then, like a sideshow magician, he snatched away the sheet and held the leg up with both hands to the moonlight, a pale symbol of the fragility of the human body and human promises. There was a long, soft "Oooohhhhhhh" from the fence. Quickly Frank laid the leg in the hole, threw in the sheet and started to shovel the dirt. When his father looked out a minute later, all he saw was a deserted fence and his son trudging back to the garden shed with the shovel.

In the good old days before movies, television, radio and the Internet, when self-reliant Americans had to entertain themselves, an amputation drew as large a crowd as a murder trial or horse race. People started gathering out front long before they brought the victim up from the tracks. Only the Doctor seemed unperturbed. He finished dinner, put on a fresh shirt and waited.

"See how calm old Doc is," they always said, straining to see in the windows.

Two generations before antibiotics, aseptic operating rooms and transfusions, the patient's confidence was the physician's best medicine. The Doctor's deep set brown eyes, huge mustache and bearing of a Civil War battlefield surgeon was more comforting to his patients than an MRI machine or the most sophisticated blood tests are today. Exuding calm, the Doctor sat on the front porch reading the paper, until the railroad men whipped the wagon up the hill with the white faced Brakeman lying wrapped in bloody blankets in the back, frozen in shock. Carefully the Doctor folded his paper and walked out to the wagon. At least this time they had remembered the blankets.

"Carry him gently," the Doctor ordered.

The driver and two railroad men lifted the Brakeman out of the wagon and followed the Doctor around the house to the side door to the operating room. The patient was a big man, over six feet tall, shrunken by pain and chills into something gray and shuddering. Frank followed proudly. As the Doctor's son, he was allowed into the bloody, painful world of men and tell his awed companions the horrors he had witnessed.

Then the crowd would wait. If the Doctor reappeared at the front door, rolling down his sleeves, they knew the patient would live. Soon the stretcher-bearers would reappear to carry their precious burden back to the tiny houses near the railroad yard. The crowd would nod and purr and shake their heads, and say what a miracle it was. If the Doctor reappeared in the side yard to lead the stretcher-bearers back around the house, though, it meant he was taking the body home to offer what comfort he could to the widow and children. Then the watchers would shake their heads solemnly, and acknowledge in whispers the inscrutable ways of God.

That night people were talking about another miracle. Turning off the gaslight, the Doctor wondered whether he should have bought a stuffed chair to match his red plush couch and operating table, when his wife interrupted his reverie.

"Samuel," she called from the door. "They need you at the Barrel Oak. Jack Townsed has been taken with apoplexy."

The Doctor started as if he had been struck.

"Townsed?" he gasped and grabbed the end of the couch to keep his balance.

For the first time since the Civil War had ended, he felt the world slide away from him. Mary touched his arm.

"Sam, what is it?"

He took her hand, and they sat down together on the couch. Her silk dress, supported by unseen cascading linens, seemed to exhale around her. Unlike her husband, who could remove his jacket after dinner at home or during surgery, she was always wrapped in clothes more confining than convention.

"He was my first amputee. It was at the battle of Chattanooga."

The Doctor ran his hand over his face.

"I had to do it."

"You should go to him."

"It wasn't that bad, Mary; a clean shot through the thigh. But I couldn't save his leg. Another doctor, one with more experience . . ."

"You gave him another fifteen years of life. It's not your fault he spent most of them in the Barrel Oak."

"Nor his, Mary."

She had kept her courage and sense of humor through four terrible years of war, and her figure through five children. The Doctor picked up his bag of sharp instruments, salves and liniments and followed her through the house to the front door.

"You can do it, Samuel," she said in the same tone as when he boarded the train for the Army.

He touched her sleeve and nodded.

"Ready, Doc?" a voice heavy with whiskey called from the porch.

"Let the Doctor drive," Mary called as the two men walked toward the buggy.

Jack Townsed was lying on a card table, breathing like a man in a race. The Doctor touched his wrist for a pulse, called to the Bartender for a bucket and started to roll up the patient's sleeve. Townsed's pink eyes fluttered open.

"That you. Doc?"

"It's me, Jack," the Doctor replied, opening his bag for the scalpel.

The patient raised his head enough to see the curved steel.

"Don't bleed me!"

He touched the Doctor's arm.

"We have to relieve the pressure on your heart, Jack."

"Bend over, Doc. There's something I got to tell you."

Townsed's eyes darted at the solemn eavesdroppers surrounding doctor and patient. The Doctor turned slowly to the onlookers, who withdrew before his commanding eyes. Then, like a priest with a penitent he leaned so close that his ear nearly touched his patient's lips.

"Bury me with two legs, Doc. I got to face God on my feet."

The Doctor recoiled.

"We lost that leg fifteen years ago."

"I know you got more, Doc. The boys say you got a whole yard full. This one thing, Sam, and I can die in peace."

No one in the Barrel Oak had ever seen tears in the Doctor's eyes before.

"All right, Jack. I'll find you a real good one."

The dying man lay back, content. As the Doctor replaced the scalpel in his bag, the habitués of the Barrel Oak marveled at how the Doctor had brought something more precious than life and more enduring than drink in his black bag of salves and scalpels.

The Doctor walked around the house to the side yard. Frank was still up; he could see the orange tip of the cigar pulsing by the fence.

"Go get your shovel, son," he called. "We have another job to do."

The orange tip winked and disappeared.

"And save the cigar. We'll need it."

When Frank returned from the shed, the Doctor relit the lantern and the cigar. Frank waited expectantly with the shovel while the Doctor took a long pull on the cigar. They both sensed that for the first time, the Doctor found it difficult to talk to his son.

"I want you to dig up the Brakeman's leg, wash it off real good, and take it to the undertaker's. He'll be waiting for you round the back, where they take the bodies," the Doctor said. "And Frank."

The Doctor wiped his eyes.

"This has to be just between us and the undertaker and Jack Townsed."

"What are they going to do with it?" Frank asked.

He suddenly realized that the world of men held more secrets than cigars and excited stories about the brothel at the far end of town.

"Jack thinks he's going to need it where he's going, and for all I know, he may be right. And here," he handed his son the cigar. "You can finish this for me."

"What were you two doing out in the garden?" Mary demanded, as her husband bumped his way into their bedroom without a candle.

"I took him into my confidence," the Doctor replied, sitting on the edge of the bed to take off his shoes.

"Does this have something to do with Jack Townsed?" she asked.

"It does," he said. "He asked me for his leg, Mary. This time I couldn't refuse him."

Mary, also, felt the world start to lift away, as it had during childbirth and the death of her mother. The little boy whom she had cared for from diapers to knickers was starting to become a man. To reach him again, she would have to work harder than when he was an infant.

Before the funeral began a day later, Frank and his father looked into Jack Townsed's casket. With a fresh haircut and shave, Jack's face looked surprisingly content over the high blue collar of the 304th Regiment of the Ohio Volunteer Infantry.

"He looks better than life," the Doctor said to the Undertaker.

The Undertaker nodded to the doctor and his son. If no one else looked too closely, they would go to their graves the only men knowing that Jack Townsed had marched to his last muster on two legs.

A month later the world had settled back on its axis. The Doctor tended births, deaths, and all the calamities between, while his wife tended him and their three sons and two daughters. Frank had not shown any particular maturity since the night of his father's shared secret. To the contrary, he seemed as immature and idiotic as ever, parading down the avenue with his friends, only to disappear whenever anyone respectable appeared. The smell of tobacco on his clothes was becoming stronger.

"You really should talk to him about smoking," Mary said to the Doctor at breakfast. "It can't be that good for him. "

The Doctor folded the newspaper and retreated to his operating room. When he found the time to talk to Frank about women, he meant to use his wife as an example of the kind not to cross.

In the days before telephones and patient reminders, the Doctor never knew who would be waiting on the long bench outside his examination and operating room. A young man, neatly dressed, turned as the Doctor approached. It was only when he saw the man's left trouser leg was sewed up at the thigh that he recognized the Brakeman. They shook hands, and the doctor was pleasantly surprised when the patient refused his offer of help into the examination room, preferring to assist himself with a crutch.

The stump had healed well, with no sign of sepsis. With quick, firm movements, the Doctor removed the stitches and washed the stump with alcohol. As the young man pulled on his trousers, the Doctor felt a surge of professional pride at having brought one more railroad man through his almost inevitable collision between flesh and steel.

"There's just one problem, Doc," the Brakeman confided, resuming the chair before the Doctor. "It itches like hell."

"Don't scratch it," the Doctor cautioned. "It could still get infected."

"It's not what's left that itches." The Brakeman paused, so he would not be misunderstood again. "It's what's gone. My left calf itches so bad I can't stand it."

"That's very common," the Doctor said sympathetically. "It's called phantom limb. In most cases, it goes away after awhile."

"It's just killing me, Doc," the Brakeman continued. "I can't sleep. I can't even think about anything else."

"There's no known cure," the Doctor explained, as he must so often, the awful helplessness of his profession.

"I think there is," the Brakeman said defiantly.

"What?"

"I've got to scratch it!"

The Doctor looked at him closely. Sometimes trauma drove people so far beyond their limits that they entered a separate world reconstructed from within to account for their pain. The young man's eyes were clear; he was not feverish or hallucinating. The Doctor felt himself sweat through his clean starched shirt.

"We had to get rid of the leg the night of the operation," the Doctor began.

"Everybody in town knows Frank buries the arms and legs out back," the Brakeman countered.

The Doctor could not meet his patient's eyes. How could he tell the Brakeman he had buried his leg with Jack Townsed?

"It wouldn't be a pretty sight," the Doctor tried to dissuade him.

"I just have to scratch it," pleaded the Brakeman. "Just once."

"All right," the Doctor said to gain time to think. "I'll call Frank. But I'm not sure where he buried it."

"We'll find it," the Brakeman said enthusiastically. "Doc, you don't know how much this means to me."

The Doctor left his excited patient and went back into the house for his son.

"Frank!" he called. "I've got a job for you."

His son had never heard that tone in his father's voice. *He found out we were peeking in the window at the brothel last Saturday night,* he thought frantically. Despite his terror, he responded quickly. It was not his sins that confronted him in the hall outside the operating room, however; it was his father's.

"Son, you've got to help me," the Doctor said, gripping Frank's arm. "The Brakeman's come for his leg."

Frank was speechless; he had never imagined that anything his father did could have a bad result.

"Listen," the Doctor said, mind racing. "Take him out back and start digging. When you find one that looks like it might fit, tell him it's his."

Frank just stared at him, his eyes asking why.

"Because he wants to scratch the damn thing!" cried the Doctor. "Now get your shovel and start digging."

All morning long, while Frank dug hole after hole, the Brakeman watched from a wrought iron chair on the terrace, shouting encouragement. Between patients, during patients, the Doctor watched his son's progress from the window. Once Frank held up the remains of a leg, cut off mid thigh just like the Brakeman's.

"Thank God," the Doctor muttered.

His patient, a young woman surprised to find herself pregnant, looked at him questioningly.

"That's a right leg," the Brakeman called. "Mine's a left."

By noon the yard was pitted with holes.

Except for a country ham, Frank had found nothing of use. The Doctor was frantic; he had never felt so helpless.

"Would you like to tell me what on earth you and your son are doing to our yard?" Mary demanded when she returned from market.

"We're trying to find the Brakeman's leg," her husband replied nervously.

"Why?"

"It itches, Mary. He wants to scratch it."

Mary looked at her husband, then out the window at her son, then started to laugh. She was still laughing when she brought lemonade to the exhausted digger and his one-legged supervisor. Her husband followed her onto the terrace and placed one of the wrought iron chairs beside the Brakeman for her.

"This is real luxury," the Brakeman said, thanking her for the lemonade. "I would have had to work forty years on the railroad to ever live like this."

Mary remained standing.

"What are you going to do with yourself now, Ben?" she asked with a hint of command in her voice.

"Well, Ma'am, the leg's been giving me so much trouble, I just haven't quite made up my mind yet."

The Doctor stood on the edge of the terrace, exchanging hopeless gestures with his son. Along the fence, Frank's friends watched, smirking.

"When I was up town today, Mr. Simpson at the bank said he was short a clerk."

As she spoke the tone of command became loud enough to quiet the idlers at the fence.

"Don't know how I could write figures all day with my leg itching the way it does."

"Oh, for heaven's sake," she exclaimed, placing her left foot onto the empty chair beside him and pulling back her silk dress. "If you have to scratch a leg, scratch mine!"

The Doctor whirled around, speechless; the Brakeman spilled his lemonade in his lap; Frank dropped his spade; and the adolescents at the fence gawked at the frothy hidden secrets that billowed up beneath the hoops of rectitude.

"Mrs. McCormick, I, I couldn't," the Brakeman stammered.

"You can and you will!" she insisted.

The Brakeman could not meet those eyes, and he could not flee. With quivering fingers, he reached out to touch the white bloomers that swelled from her thigh to her black high button shoe. As if the linen were the spikes of a poisonous insect, he jerked back his hand.

"Now, Mary," the Doctor began.

"Go ahead. Do it!" she snapped.

From the lawn, Frank saw his father step back, and in that second he realized there were powers not possessed by mere men and secrets that could never be learned in a lifetime at the Barrel Oak. Swallowing hard, the Brakeman reached out again and started to scratch her calf.

"Harder!" she commanded. "Good!"

Then she set her foot back on the terrace, and the skirt dropped like a curtain at the end of the last act.

"How's that?" she demanded. "Better?"

"Yes, Ma'am," the Brakeman agreed. "Better than I felt before the accident."

"Good. Now Frank," she called to her son. "Get

those worthless friends of yours and help Ben to the Doctor's buggy and drive him home."

"Mrs. McCormick, Ma'am, I don't know how to thank you," the Brakeman said, as the boys lifted him into the seat beside Frank.

"You'll thank me best by seeing Mr. Simpson first thing tomorrow morning about that job and finding yourself a decent woman to marry."

"Yes, Ma' am," he replied.

Frank clicked the horse into motion. The other boys glanced at the Doctor's wife and scattered to their homes with the awful recognition that their own mothers and possibly even other women they were fated to meet might also be capable of decisive action.

Her husband touched her arm as their son drove away.

"A most unusual cure for phantom limb," he said admiringly.

"I trust I will not have to intrude on your province again," she replied.

"Nor I on yours, Mary," he said.

She looked up at him quickly with the same smile that had captivated him at the parade when his regiment had been deactivated fifteen years earlier. Together they walked around the house to the garden and sat laughing and talking until their son returned and started to fill in the holes in the back yard.

BREAKING
COVER

Everyone said the dog hunted better in Mike's stories than in the field. I only saw her, a whitish-yellow mixture of setter and lab disoriented by the spoor of chewing gum on hot concrete, once before he died. In his ragged beard and jeans, Mike looked as out of place in the city as his dog. He had brought her from the farm to watch him work on a brief, but she took him for a walk instead. As he told me the bear story for the tenth time, I knew that the brief would be filed late or not at all. Mike was always about to write the great bird-hunting story, too, but he told them better than he wrote them, because he never wrote them.

When I first read the obituary, I thought it was about somebody else. Nothing matched my memory of him with the dog, gesturing with the leash in his left hand, while his right arm, shrunken by polio and surgery, swung from his T-shirt. They used his full name, Frederick Michael Jaeger, the way he signed court papers, and eulogized him as an old fashioned lawyer dedicated to the rights of the poor. I only knew him as Mike, and he represented poor people because they made the least demands on him. It wasn't until the afternoon, when a friend who rented him office space called, that I realized that Frederick Michael Jaeger was the bird hunter.

His family was from the Southwest. Because Mike had borrowed from them to pay his office rent, they had the landlord's number. His brother wanted another lawyer to go through Mike's files so none of his cases went into default. My friend paused. After my divorce, I got a lot of calls to fill in for other people. I said I could do it over the weekend.

"Great," he said. "They're going to bury him at the farm Friday afternoon. His brother said you can stay over."

Everyone who knew Mike was at the funeral except the dog, who had gone off to grieve alone. I recognized the landlord and a few criminal defense attorneys, but the farmers and hunters and the brother from Texas were strangers. For me Mike was the would-be writer; for his brother, the kid twisted away from his roots and success by a childhood disease; for the farmers and hunters, the best good old boy his adopted county had ever known.

The funeral home had dug the grave in an old family plot thirty yards behind the house. It wasn't Mike's family, but he had loved the place so much he would fit in as well as he had anywhere else. After the service, we drank lemonade from concentrate on the back porch and told the kind of stories that make people laugh at funerals. Lemonade wasn't the bird hunter's drink, but the only minister they could find was a Baptist, who had not known Mike.

The story everyone knew best was the bear story. To prove it was true, a farmer called the dog to show her scars, but she didn't answer. Everyone had seen them: four ugly welts on her back and right side, where the bear had slashed her just before Mike fired.

"No, this is how it really happened," a hunter said and started all over again. Depending on who was telling it, the story was either hysterically funny or more frightening than a recurring nightmare.

Mike was hunting quail on a gray October afternoon, following the dog through the field along the creek and up into the scrub. Several years earlier, he had sold half the timber on the hillside, and weeds and brush had taken over. To conceal his need for money, he told everyone he cut the trees to create cover for quail. Only the hunters believed him.

It had been a long, cold, frustrating day; he had only had one shot and missed. The dog swept back and forth across the hillside and into a gully, where the wind turned around and blew over them toward the woods. They were close enough that he could see a spittle of snow swirling against the dark trees. He was about to turn back when the dog went on point. Mike crept forward, knowing she had found game.

Then he saw the covey staring straight at him from behind a brown grass veil, the only movement the swelling of their chests. You could hunt twenty years and not have a moment like this. Because of his weak right arm, Mike used a single shot 410 shotgun and had to plan every shot. This time he knew where they would fly before they broke and was leaning into the shot when splat! He slipped in the worst stinking mess he had ever seen and sat down hard, firing into the empty sky.

Mike couldn't figure out how a cow could have been in the gully, or what the cow could have eaten that smelled so vile. It was so fresh it hadn't set.

"Damn it!" he said, wiping his boot in the stubble and calling the dog. "We're going home."

She was just turning when she pointed again, straight toward the woods. Mike couldn't believe it. He should have spooked everything for miles around. But no, the dog had spotted something. Cradling the shotgun on his weak right arm, he broke and reloaded it with his left hand. The dog let him get even with her when he saw them again, watching from behind the grass.

"Go!" he told her, and she leapt ahead.

With a rush like a thousand dragonflies the birds burst out of the grass and dove toward the trees. Mike fired, and a quail snapped to the side and careened into the woods.

"Go get him!" he called to the dog, angry with himself for a bad shot. The quail was flapping furiously behind the trees. As the dog bounded into the woods, he reloaded. Maybe I should give up shooting, he thought. Just run the dogs for the other guys. He could aim the shotgun with his left hand, but his right was so weak he often missed or worse, just wounded a bird.

The dog bolted from the woods, mouth empty.

"Now what the hell?" he thought, glad no one else was with him to see the bird hunter's ultimate disgrace: a dog that would not hunt. She jumped against his chest like a terrified child, trying to turn him around.

"What the hell is it?" he cried, staring into the woods.

A piece of darkness moved between the trees. With the wind behind them, neither dog nor hunter had known what was lurking there, but it had been tracking them by their smell for an hour.

"Oh, shit!"

The bear charged out of the woods straight at them, eight hundred pounds of galloping hate. Mike started to run, but the dog sprang toward the bear and leapt at its throat. Like a man brushing away a mosquito, the bear knocked it aside. That was enough time for Mike to aim at its face and fire.

"The bear cried like a child and sat down hard," everyone on the porch said laughing.

That was the one line that was always the same. Then the bear arched on its feet like a Sumo wrestler and lunged at the stench of the man. One side of its face was an open wound, and a drunken yellow eye rolled madly in the other. Mike ran from the hot breath closing behind him and damn! He slipped on the bear shit again and fell flat on his back. Like a lineman missing a tackle, the bear plunged over him and landed in a heap.

"I can't breathe," Mike thought. "I can't move. It's already killed me."

Something licked his neck. Mike closed his eyes and waited to die. Then it licked his eyes. It was the dog, telling him to get his ass up and moving while the bear was upwind. Shrieking and roaring, it rolled and slashed at the stubble. Mike stood up and lurched to the side. The bear heard him and stood up, sniffing the cold air for the man. The dog darted forward and yapped at its heels, turning it around. Disoriented, it missed their scent. Mike and the dog ran in a long arch away back to the creek, while the bear stood raging at the winter sky.

"That dog trusted Mike so much she let him sew her up," the hunter said.

That night Mike slept by the door with his 12 gauge loaded with deer slugs in case the bear picked up their scent and followed them home.

"He'd never go near the woods again," one of the farmers said.

I looked over the field toward the hillside, where the trees angled down into the scrub.

"He said he could hear it out there," John said. "One night it came so close he could smell it."

"In his dreams," the hunter said.

"Only time I ever seen bear shit was right on the other side of that barn," the farmer countered, and everybody laughed again.

"I just wish he had written about it," my friend the landlord said, a touch of anger in his voice. "The son of a bitch could have been a great writer."

"It was an accident," a lawyer said to calm him. "It's not anybody's fault."

"That's what makes me so damn mad," the landlord said. "There's nothing anybody could do to change it."

Then it was time to go, and the farmers' pickups, the lawyers' cars, and the hunters' utility vehicles lumbered out of the yard onto the gravel driveway.

"That's where it happened," the farmer told me, pointing in front of the house. Mike had just turned onto the old state road when the other driver swerved around a stopped car and hit him head-on. He was dead before they got him to the hospital.

I told Mike's brother I'd take the active case files to my office Monday. He was getting into a rental car to return to the airport when I asked about the dog.

"I can't keep her in my apartment," I said.

"I'm talking to some of the hunters," he replied. "I'll call when something's firmed up."

I got my suitcase out of my 4x4 and went to the house to change. Everyone was gone; the women from the church had cleaned up the lemonade and left. A heavy

Ohio afternoon with hardly any air hung over the old brick house, as it had every summer since before the Civil War. The screen door slammed so loud I expected Mike to come running down the stairs yelling, "Who the hell's there?"

It was musty inside, as if the occupant left the windows open in the rain. The only twentieth-century improvements were linoleum in the kitchen and a tub and toilet in the upstairs bathroom. I changed into jeans and T-shirt in Mike's bedroom. His stories about the bedroom were nearly as good as the ones about the dog and probably about as true. Of the women at the funeral, only my friend's wife had wept. His drawer and closet were open, where he'd grabbed his clothes for court Tuesday morning just before he turned onto the road.

In the living room Mike's files were piled on a desk and on the floor, entangled in computer and stereo cables. He had talked a lot about the computer, how he was going to use it to organize his practice. He had even bought a voice recognition device to take down his stories live. When I tried to turn the computer on, nothing happened. He did not get any farther than taking it out of the box.

The shotguns, though, were in perfect order. He had them displayed on handmade racks on the wall. Here was his beloved 410, a high school graduation gift from his father, and all the others that gift had spawned. A twelve gauge rested against the wall by his chair. I hefted it and checked the magazine. Sure enough, he had four deer slugs in the tube and one in the chamber, as if that bear were coming back any minute.

His files were slim. Mike didn't take a case where he had to write much. That's why he practiced criminal law, where he could plea bargain with the prosecutors or try to draw the jurors off the scent with a good story about the defendant's grandmother. He might have been a great lawyer when lawyers still practiced with the spoken word, before the word processor and copying machine made it too easy to spew words onto paper and stifle the human voice with ink.

In the early evening, after I had gone through the active cases, the dog came home. I heard her outside, whining and pawing the screen. There was a sack of dog food behind the door and a bowl on the porch. While I poured she stood back, wondering who I was. She had so many burrs and scratches she must have slept out since Mike died.

The refrigerator was what I expected: beer, eggs, a half loaf of bread turning blue at the edges, hardening cheese, lunch meat, and half a solidified burrito wrapped in wax paper. I made a cheese sandwich, took a beer, and sat out on the porch with the dog. I could have gone back that night, but if I stayed, somebody might call about the dog.

For a long time she stared at me from across the porch, trying to place me. Finally remembering some dim connection with Mike, she slouched over, sat down and let me remove the burrs. Pulling apart her fur, I saw the crisscross stitches over her scars where Mike had sewn her up. Then she whined to go in. Still looking for Mike, I thought, and opened the screen for her. She went inside and turned around, signaling me to follow. Then she led me to the cupboard where he kept the bourbon.

"All right, old girl" I said. "We'll have a drink together."

I filled a glass with frost-encrusted ice, picked up the bottle and followed her back to the porch. Here was the reason so many briefs were late and so many great stories never written.

The sun setting over the hills made me understand it wasn't a bad choice. As the sky darkened, the glow from the afternoon lingered over the corn, then slowly slipped away around the house. The trees on the hill blurred into dark green and black, rising to cover the orange sun. With night everything moved closer: the barn, the old graves, the trees stretching down to the scrub. The dog didn't move when I went in for more ice.

She was pacing when I came back outside. I reached out and called her, but she growled softly to be still and sniffed the night air. I sat down beside her on the step. She wouldn't let me touch her. The moon had risen over the house, silhouetting the barn and the graveyard against the blackness like a weak x-ray.

What do they sense in the air that we miss, I wondered, sipping the ice-cold bourbon. What wonders or dangers lie just beyond our senses? Reach out and peel away the night, and you will see choirs of angels shimmering over the fields. Suddenly she bared her teeth and stared into the dark, as if expecting a devil to leap out.

"Come on, old girl," I said. "Relax. We'll have just one more and go to bed."

Then I smelled it, too, something rank and poisonous like an infected wound oozing through the heavy air. The dog froze. A cloud covered the moon, and everything went black. When the light returned, something large as death had separated from the hillside and was slouching toward us through the field. Had it smelled him in the grave and thought it had finally caught its old enemy away from the house after dark? I could see the bear clearly now, looming over the old tombstones. With a wild cry the dog leapt off the porch and charged it.

It swatted the dog to earth so hard she didn't get up. It didn't smell me, or confused my scent with the departed mourners. Snorting, panting, it went down on all fours and started to dig up his grave. I felt my way into the house and eased the screen door shut. Mike's twelve gauge glowed in the moonlight through the window. So the story wasn't a drunken nightmare; this was why the bird hunter kept it by his chair at night. I slipped off the safety and went outside.

It was head down in the grave, like a devil digging its way back to hell. With a scream like a dying child, its claws scraped the casket.

"Stand up, you bastard!" I yelled.

Sniffing and slobbering, it rose from the grave, furious at the interruption. The swollen eye rolled in the moonlight until it focused on me. Then it caught my scent and bounded toward me faster than a fat man in a bar fight.

It was so low my first shot missed, the second grazed its back and the third broke a front leg, rolling it toward the porch. Then the twelve gauge jammed. Roaring, the bear stood up on its haunches, thrashing the air, and I stared into the festered wound and yellow eye.

"God," I thought. "God!"

I pushed and pulled the pump as it lurched forward, step by step, like lingering death. Its hot breath choked me. Then something moved behind it. Like a specter from the grave, the old white dog dragged herself forward on her front legs and fell on the bear's right heel. Bellowing, it turned on her, just as the empty shell sprang out of the chamber.

"Damn you!" I screamed as I fired the last two slugs into its head. Damn the accident and the evil and everything else that keeps a man from being himself. The bear reared up, swung one last time at the night and collapsed.

The dog was much smaller, dying. I knelt beside her and stroked her heaving shoulder. She was so happy. I rested my hand on her muzzle until she stopped breathing.

Then I went to Mike's grave. The bear had torn the lid off the coffin. Like a sinner trying to escape on judgment day, the bird hunter was half in and half out. I climbed down and laid him back on the satin liner. Then I picked up his dog and placed her on his chest. The lid wouldn't fit, but they didn't need it to separate them from the earth. They would be much happier returning to dust together.

I found a shovel in the barn and dug until the old house was rosy in the morning sun. Then back to the barn for a chain. I looped the chain around the bear's hind leg, fastened the end to the tow on my 4x4 and dragged the carcass to the grave. Pushing, heaving, cursing it as much in death as in life, I finally tumbled it into the pit. Its shattered, shapeless face caught against the side. Like a demon that would not die, it grinned at me with long yellow teeth. I kicked it over the edge. Still cursing, I shoveled dirt over it until it was covered forever.

I didn't really understand Mike until I stood in his shower with the stench of death and hate streaming off me. For him, everything besides bird hunting was an extra. He had lived his own way until the accident or the evil that catches us all found him. But he had lived.

The phone awakened me in the afternoon. I didn't answer. It was probably the brother or a hunter calling about the dog, and I didn't want to explain. I took Mike's files, locked the back door and went to my car. Someday an archeologist may find them and wonder whether people at the end of the twentieth century sacrificed animals at the tombs of their kings. That's not a bad way to remember a man, even if he never wrote his own story.

NOT UNTIL
EVERYTHING'S
PERFECT

The one time I met the Ashleys, I never imagined they would try to reverse the world and carry us back to Eden. They had just purchased the three story fieldstone house on the double lot cater-corner across the street from ours. Tall, thin, late fifties, in matching khaki shorts, white socks and athletic shoes, they were inventorying their trees with the enthusiasm of beginning botany students on a wooded campus. Behind them, like a college dormitory, loomed the huge L-shaped structure they would never inhabit.

He watched me approach with the slightly condescending smile of a man accustomed to being called "Sir" by thirty-year-old MBAs.

"When are you going to move in?" I asked, after the briefest introductions.

He lowered his clipboard, and she her illustrated arboreal guide, to stare at me. I had not thought it so difficult a question. Then Robert Ashley turned to his platinum-haired wife, who smiled as pleasantly as if she were meeting a new masseur.

"Not until everything's perfect," she said.

That was the first warm day in April, when the oaks were beginning to bud, and the bluebells along the curving drive still seemed too frail to have pierced the cold earth. Several weeks later, a tree service arrived with trucks and cranes to begin a summer-long clearing of underbrush and deadwood.

Another neighbor had not been as fortunate as the sellers of the Ashleys' house. Eager to retire to Florida, the owners of the adjoining property had had their house on the market for over a year. Both lots were oversize, leaving enough space to subdivide and build another house between them.

In the fall a rumor began that the Ashleys had tried to buy the extra land from their absent neighbors, but had been rebuffed. Some said Robert Ashley wanted to build a pool at the edge of his forest; others said he wanted a buffer zone to preserve his privacy. Suddenly the "For Sale" sign came down across the street, and one sentence in the Sunday real estate section reported our neighbors had sold the entire property to an attorney as trustee for an undisclosed purchaser. Discreet inquiries at the club confirmed that the purchaser was Robert Ashley.

Now there were two empty houses across the street. Oddly, the Ashleys did not put their second house back on the market. When I asked one of our real estate people to check at the courthouse, she reported that the Ashleys had not subdivided their new property to add a portion to their original lot. Were they planning on keeping both parcels?

That first winter was exceptionally hard. Several of the Ashleys' freshly-manicured trees cracked in an ice storm, calling out an emergency response team from the tree service. A large stone from the retaining wall that framed their lot like the foundation of a temple tumbled into the sidewalk. Blue service trucks from the gas company, the telephone company, and interior contractors slid up and down the driveway, but the Ashleys did not move in.

In the spring the tree service returned to clear away the ravages of winter. Contractors arrived again in force, some with exotic names and emblems stenciled on their vans, others in old trucks piled high with tools and ladders. A lawn service visited the grounds weekly to prune, fertilize and cut. Old shutters came down, new shutters went up, and on the hottest days of summer, workers sweated on the searing tin roof. Chimneys were tuck-pointed; jacks temporarily replaced the wooden columns on the huge front porch, while the originals were sanded, repainted, and restored. Still the Ashleys did not move in.

The neighbor on the far side of the Ashleys was doing some renovations, too. Over lunch at the club he told me about a call from Robert Ashley's attorney.

"He said Mr. Ashley didn't like the addition and what we were doing with the gardens," Erickson fumed. "So I asked him, 'What the hell business is it of Ashley's?' And the lawyer tells me, 'Mr. Ashley wants everything to be perfect.'"

Neither Erickson nor I had ever heard of such an encounter. No demand, no threat of legal action, just an expression that the Ericksons were not living up to the Ashleys' standards of perfection.

That was the second winter we had two empty houses across the street. One Sunday morning the dog bounded into the bedroom and barked wildly at the window.

"See what he wants," my wife said without opening her eyes.

I stood up and parted two levolors® with my fingers. Beneath the Ashleys' leafless oaks were five butternut gray deer facing different directions, like a foraging party of Confederate cavalry. The leader, a five point buck, slowly turned his head past two does and two fawns.

"What are you looking at?" Lillian demanded, turning toward me.

I wish now I had said: "Nothing, dear. It's just the newspaper." Lillian always pretended to be stronger than she was.

Instead I whispered, "Come here. Don't say anything."

Not quite believing that I could recognize anything that might interest her, she got out of bed and came to the window.

"I don't see anything. Where?"

Just as the two black eyes fixed on us, she moved the levolors. With a toss of his head, the buck turned his marauders away, and they sauntered off after him through the trees.

"They must have come up from the river," she exclaimed.

In church that morning, the Old Testament lesson was about wild animals overrunning Israel during a time of desolation. Were the Ashleys' deer a portent of some disaster that would depopulate the city and leave it in ruins and to the ravages of nature? Lillian's interest deepened to the point of obsession. Why, she kept asking, would anyone buy two homes and leave them like doll houses across the street from us? As if to dispel her fears, however, the contractors and tree service and yard men returned the third summer in even greater force. The Ashleys, however, did not move in.

One evening that fall while she was out walking the dog, Lillian saw a black Jaguar in front of the Ashleys'. Curious, she went up the long, dark driveway. Only the porch light and a light in the third story were on. Stepping back under the trees, she saw the silhouettes of a man and a woman against the third floor blinds and heard their angry voices.

Only two words were recognizable. Over and over again, the woman repeated: "The wallpaper! The wallpaper!"

Suddenly the upstairs light went out. Lillian ran down the driveway, pulling the terrified dog after her.

"What was it?" I asked when she stood weeping in the kitchen.

"The Ashleys were floating down the stairs after me," she sobbed.

"You've never met the Ashleys," I protested. "How could you recognize them?"

"It was the Ashleys," she insisted.

"But you were outside," I tried to reason with her. "You couldn't see the stairs."

"You never believe me," she cried, turning away. "I know what I saw."

That was when she stopped talking to me and started to spend most of her time alone. I had always known she was delicate, but never thought one unexpected touch could break her. It was several months before her friends stopped calling. One day in January, she left me a note that she was taking the dog to the veterinarian; she just couldn't stand its whining anymore. When I called the veterinarian to bring him home, they said they had already disposed of the remains.

At the office, in the long, empty evenings at home, at church, when I awoke at night, I thought about the Ashleys. What, to them, was perfection? Wallpaper? Landscaping? Ductwork? Or was their vision like the ancient Hebrews, who believed that the Messiah would come if every Jew followed the Law for just one day? What did the Ashleys require of us?

The next spring our neighbor up the street was suddenly transferred to Denver. They were so happy to get their asking price that they didn't tell us that the buyer was the Ashleys' attorney as trustee. The week they moved, Lillian had to go into the hospital. The doctors were hopeful; there were many treatment strategies; with time they were sure to find the right one for her.

Time brought the rumor that Erickson, whose addition had provoked Robert Ashley's wrath, was in financial trouble and would have to give up his house. For weeks I dreaded opening the Sunday paper to read the real estate transfers. At Thanksgiving the rumor proved true: the Ashleys' attorney had acquired another home.

That is why I did not protest when the doctors suggested sending Lillian to an institution in the state capitol for long-term care. Those sallow, green-walled cubicles are no less conducive to recovery than a neighborhood of empty houses. I still drive up to see her on weekends when the weather is good.

During those drives I finally understood the Ashleys' concept of perfection: a world cleansed of all corrupt humanity as it was before the creation of Adam and Eve. We could not be converted to the Ashleys' vision; Erickson had proved that. We had to be expelled from a garden as fragile as Eden that could only support two inhabitants.

Whether the Ashleys can create a world more perfectly than God I do not know. The older couple down the street is talking about moving to a condominium. That will leave our house as the only inhabited dwelling to face the Ashleys'. It really doesn't make much sense to keep it without Lillian. I am almost comforted to know there will be no problem finding a buyer.

THE RESURRECTION
OF NELSON CAMPBELL

"Nelson's back in the hospital again," Elizabeth Campbell said. "You have to come right away." The call from the sixty-two year old widow interrupted Charles Spears, Rector of the Downtown Church of' Our Savior, as he was preparing his sermon on the raising of Lazarus from the dead.

"Which unit?" he asked automatically. After preaching for forty years on the same text, Spears was unable to think of a new approach to the miracle.

"Intensive care. Can you meet me there?"

From the crackling on the phone, Elizabeth was calling from her cell.

"Yes. Of course," the priest replied.

"Thank God. I can't go through this again by myself."

When inspiration failed, Spears, like many of his aging colleagues, considered repeating sermons from decades past that no one in his current parish had heard. But where had he stored his sermon notes from the 1970s? As the priest was getting into his car, he remembered that Nelson Campbell had died in intensive care five years earlier.

Like an architectural rendering from the old Soviet Union, the hospital sprawled over several city blocks. Hundreds of one-way glass windows, hermetically sealed to keep patients and air and souls from escaping, checkered the concrete slab façade. Maybe Nelson Campbell had been wandering through forgotten corridors for five years in his split-back hospital gown, trying to find the exit. But Nelson Campbell had been cremated, and Spears himself had interred his ashes in the columbarium behind the altar.

Spears parked three levels down from physicians' parking. Following the signs to intensive care, he passed a large room half lit by television sets where dull-eyed people sat on vinyl couches drinking carbonated beverages. This is how I will find Elizabeth, he thought, holding her older daughter's hand, staring at the floor while the reflection from a television plays across her empty face. A whispered explanation from the doctor, a hug and frightened good-byes, then a big-boned woman would arrive to escort poor Mrs. Campbell to her new quarters in the psychiatry wing. Thus would begin the normal progression of his older parishioners from condo or assisted living to the linoleum-floored Alzheimer's unit at the Episcopal Retirement Home.

Elizabeth was standing beside the cardiologist at the nurse's station looking at Nelson's old records on a monitor. Wearing a dark suit that contrasted expensively with her layered blond hair, she seemed strangely out of place, like Condoleezza Rice in a Baghdad bunker.

"It can't be Nelson," she insisted. "It just can't be."

"Everything checks out from the last time," the cardiologist said. "The scar from the old appendectomy, the mole over the left eyebrow, the incisions from the knee operation, even bruising from the IV lines."

"My God," Elizabeth shuddered.

"He's exactly the same as he was before he went into ventricular fibrillation," the physician continued.

"Thank God you're here," Elizabeth said to the priest. "I can't go in there by myself."

Across the corridor they could see the lower part of a draped body lit by blinking bedside monitors.

"What happened?" wondered Spears.

"A nurse found him," the cardiologist said. "She called a 'Code Blue,' and this time they were able to revive him."

"Has anyone talked to him?" Spears asked.

"He's still a little groggy," the cardiologist replied, glancing at Spears' clerical collar. "We don't see many cases like this."

"Neither do we," said the priest.

The Rector took his parishioner's hand, and they followed the doctor into the room. Elizabeth squeezed his fingers so hard that he grimaced. Nelson Campbell was staring at them from the bed. As he aged, his cheekbones and nose became prominent, so that his hard, angry eyes stared at them from a face like the marble head of a Roman senator.

"Hello, Betty," he said thickly. "What took you so long?"

"We just heard you were here," the priest answered for her.

"Where else would I be?" he said irritably. "I've had the strangest dreams."

"It's the anesthesia," explained the cardiologist.

Nelson looked at the doctor as if he didn't believe him.

"You look worried," he said to his wife. "Something happen to one of the kids?"

Their older daughter's husband had left her as soon as their two children reached puberty, and their son had been fired from his third job in four years. The younger daughter was staying at her mother's Naples condo seeking literary inspiration after two DUIs in one quarter and dropping out of the creative writing program at City University.

"Everybody's just fine, Nelson," she replied with a frozen smile.

"I'm tired, Betty," he said, closing his eyes. "Come back later. And Charles, we have to talk."

"Yes," said the priest. "I'd like that."

While the cardiologist fussed with the monitors to provide cover, Nelson Campbell's widow and clergyman left the room.

"It was such a lovely funeral," she said, dabbing her eyes with a tissue.

Like most wealthy widows, her husband's death had been a profound relief, terminating the random emotional violence of a thirty-five year marriage and leaving her with the spoils of his ruthless business career. Returning to the garage, Spears understood why people awaited the results of their loved one's surgery so far from the operating room. They were not afraid of hearing that the operation had failed; they were afraid of hearing that it had succeeded and that the patient would return to inflict on them again the awful burden of their life.

The year before Nelson died, the church had installed a columbarium behind the altar with veneered receptacles like safe deposit boxes to hold the ashes of the dead. For Nelson Campbell, internment in a safe deposit box would have been a fitting end to an existence spent in unrestrained acquisition.

The Rector entered the chancel and crossed himself. A dark square had opened in the columbarium. The priest turned on the overhead light that illuminated the altar during the Eucharist. Sure enough, the panel that had marked the final resting place for Nelson's ashes was open. Lying on the floor, lid ajar, was his pewter urn. Spears picked it up and turned it so that the light shined inside. It was as clean as if it had never been used. Spears placed it very carefully on the altar like a chalice awaiting the sacrament.

That evening the Rector called on Mrs. Campbell at her condo overlooking the river. Daughter Meredith greeted him at the door without enthusiasm. After a casserole procured at her grocery and wine from a waxed paper box that Nelson Jr. had picked up at a drive through, the family was ready to address their patriarch's resurrection with their spiritual, legal and financial advisors. As he followed Meredith to the living room, he heard her two teenagers experimenting with the television to see just how loud they could get it before their mother shrieked at them.

"We closed the estate two years ago, Elizabeth;" Harris Scintilton, the family attorney, was trying to explain. "The company's gone. We had to sell it to diversify your portfolio."

Envisioning her husband's reaction, Elizabeth Campbell shuddered.

It was one of the few times that the well dressed lawyer welcomed the priest's presence. Spears had made him the church's Chancellor to better discern the lawyer's raids on his parishioners' estates. Mrs. Campbell motioned for Spears to take the chair across from the lawyer and next to Nelson Jr. Neither lawyer nor son stood up to greet him.

"We'd be a lot better off if you hadn't let Horlach Spencer invest the proceeds," Scintilton said to deflect his client's anger from himself to the her financial advisor.

"Will Monica be coming up from Naples?" Spears asked to break the tension, hoping the answer would be no.

"I left a message on her cell," her mother said, looking nervously at her son.

"She's probably out on the pier fishing, wouldn't you think, Meredith?" Nelson Jr. said provocatively to his sister. "I hope she cleans up her catch before she brings him home."

He was wearing jeans, a T-shirt that said "Viva Las Vegas" and dirty tennis shoes, a uniform that identified him as a habitué of bright, frothy coffee shops where customers sipped lattes and networked away the endless days.

"Just shut up!" Meredith replied, turning to shriek at her children.

If she were not sixty pounds overweight and gaining, the clothes her mother bought her on their weekly shopping sprees might have made her appear attractive. But after two children and a contested divorce, even the most lavish facial could not smooth the fault lines of rage and frustration.

"I asked Charles to discuss our situation with us," Mrs. Campbell began in the tone of the mid-twentieth-century matriarch that she had learned from her mother. "Nelson, won't you offer Mr. Spears a glass of wine?"

"Isn't Horlach coming?" Nelson Jr. interjected. "The problem is money, not miracles."

"Exactly," said Harris Scintilton.

"We've had enough miracles," his sister agreed.

The siblings looked at each other in surprise. It was the first time they had agreed on anything in years.

The doorbell rang, and the two manic grandchildren ran to open it.

"Ciao, Betty," a voice smoothed by sycophancy and alcohol called from the alcove.

"We thought you were the pizza," one of the teenagers piped.

Spears sipped the wine and quickly set down the glass. Horlach Spencer entered the living room with the same expression of eager expectation he wore as he cruised the undercroft Sunday mornings searching for the newest widow on whom to lavish his obsequies. Thanks to a superb dye job and weekly massages at the athletic club, the financial adviser exuded the sullen grace of a country club trophy winner in some indeterminate class. Betty Campbell stood to receive his embrace, and Spears shook his soft hand. The lawyer remained seated.

"What a surprise to have Nelson back," Spencer exclaimed, accepting a brim-full glass from Nelson Jr. "I can't imagine what this must mean for Betty. And you too, Harris."

"It means we're back to having Daddy dole out the money, unless you have some other suggestion," Nelson Jr. said angrily.

"That could be a problem," Horlach said, sitting down carefully on the couch next to Nelson's former widow. "Everything is tied up in those damned trusts that Harris wrote."

"Those trusts saved millions in estate taxes," Scintilton seethed.

"And generated nearly as much in fees," retorted the financial advisor.

The Rector noticed that Horlach wasn't wearing socks. Betty Campbell smoothed her skirt expectantly and gazed at him. Their hands were close enough to touch. Spears recalled persistent rumors that Spencer sometimes provided his clients with other personal services under the rubric of wealth management.

"Well, he can't have any of my money," Meredith snapped. "I've got the kids to look after by myself."

"I'm very illiquid at the moment myself," Nelson Jr. said.

"I'm sure Mr. Spencer has thought this all through," his mother said hopefully.

"Of course he'll be living with you, Betty," Spencer suggested to test her reaction. "As long as you share a car, I don't think any radical changes have to be made."

"Daddy never shared anything with anybody," Meredith laughed. "He's going to want everything back."

"You did the funeral," Nelson Jr. rounded on Charles Spears. "What went wrong?"

The priest was amazed at how quickly they moved from self-pity to clerical malpractice. Harris Scintilton eyed him like a cobra sizing up a mongoose.

"The resurrection of the dead is an article of faith," he replied.

"But not one at a time," Nelson Jr. argued. "Not just to us. It's not fair."

Tired of the TV game, the grandchildren entered the room, pouting for pizza.

"We'll get it on the way home," their mother said standing up.

"I'd better be going, too," Spears said, preferring an elevator ride with Meredith and her children to further complaints about the miracle. He left the attorney and the financial advisor eyeing each other like gauchos in a knife fight.

Elizabeth took him aside at the door, while Meredith stalked after her children to the elevator.

"What am I supposed to do if he wants to, well, you know," she whispered.

"However you handled it before, I suppose," the bachelor priest replied.

Elizabeth Campbell started to cry.

"It isn't that bad, is it'?" Spears said.

"Sometimes you just don't know what to believe, do you?" she sobbed.

Nelson was sitting up in bed against an avalanche of pillows when Spears arrived at his room.

"Oh, hi, Charles," the patient greeted him, raising an arm trailing plastic tubes. "Betty dropped by again yesterday evening. Nobody seems very happy to have me back."

"Most people have difficulty dealing with a new situation," Spears explained. "By the way, do you remember what happened?"

"Honest to God, Charlie, it was the damnedest thing I ever saw. One minute a doctor was pounding on my chest and the next I was on stage facing the lights, like when you're in junior high school choir. Everybody was wearing white robes, and we were packed in so tight on the risers that you could hardly move."

Nelson Campbell paused as if he saw again that heavenly choir surrounding him like ice sheets on a glacier facing the morning sun.

"And it just went on and on. I never could stand church music, that's why I played golf most Sundays, and now you have to stand there and sing twenty-four seven. My back was just killing me. We sang 'Swing Low, Sweet Chariot,' 'Amazing Grace,' 'The Hallelujah Chorus,' and the rest of them so damn many times I had them all memorized."

Campbell reached for a plastic cup with a bent straw and sipped.

"How did you get back here?" the priest prompted him.

"I started moving up the risers, step by step, just like I did in choir. I knew they had to end somewhere, and I could climb down and get away, maybe have a cigarette in the rest room. It seemed like it was taking me forever. I was squeezing between the two fattest women I'd ever seen, when I popped out the back."

"Popped out the back?" Spears repeated, amazed.

"I fell so far I thought I'd bust something when I landed. But here I was again with some guy pounding on my chest as if I'd never been away."

His description of heaven was unlike any Spears had ever heard. Perhaps, he thought, that was why so few return to say anything about it.

"I'm beginning to think I made a mistake," Campbell continued.

"What would you do if you returned to heaven'?" Spears wondered.

"Do you think they'd give me another chance?"

"There's always another chance," the priest assured him.

"I'd go down into the lights to the stage instead of backing out. There has to be somebody watching who can tell me what it's all about."

It was the first time Nelson Campbell had ever shown any spiritual insight. The priest was astounded. Nelson had learned nothing in his first life of sixty-seven years and everything in his second life of just one day.

"Hello, dear," Elizabeth called with forced cheerfulness from the door. "The children are here."

Meredith's children, carrying extra-large soft drinks, squeezed past her, followed by their mother and Nelson Jr.

"Let Grandma have the chair," Meredith snapped at her son, who had plopped down in the visitor's chair as soon as Spears stood up.

Nelson Campbell eyed his family with the watchfulness of a cornered animal.

"Where's Monica?" he demanded.

"We'll talk about that, Dad," Nelson Jr.. smirked. "But first we should go over the figures. Why don't you kids take a hike?"

His niece and nephew turned to their Mother.

"Where can they go?" she asked.

"There's a TV room by the lobby," Spears suggested, anxious to avoid the coming confrontation. "I'll show them."

"Come back tomorrow," Nelson said. "Sometimes I think you're the only one not trying to get something out of me."

Brushing aside the tubes, Spears shook his parishioner's hand. Meredith's children were in the elevator before he could say goodbye to Mrs. Campbell.

"You've what?" were the last words Spears heard Nelson Campbell utter just before the elevator doors closed.

Spears had just left the teenagers to fight over the largest chair in front of the waiting room TV, when he heard soft chimes signaling a "Code Blue" on the hospital intercom. Somewhere another patient was trying to escape, like a bee from a smoking hive. Did they need an alto, a tenor, or a bass in that celestial choir where Nelson Campbell was supposed to spend eternity?

There was a voice mail for him from Elizabeth Campbell when he returned to the church. Nelson had gone into ventricular fibrillation again and died. She wanted a private funeral and no obituary to draw attention to the family's misadventure with immortality. Her voice sounded much relieved.

"I hope you got it right this time," Nelson Jr. said to the priest after his father's second funeral.

Only Mrs. Campbell, Nelson Jr., Meredith and her children, Harris Scintilton, and Horlach Spencer, the people who had a real interest in keeping Nelson Campbell dead, had attended. Spears read the first draft of his sermon on the raising of Lazarus, confident that none of them would be in church to hear it again on Sunday. Once a week was enough for Episcopalians.

"Charles, there's something I wanted to ask about your sermon," Mrs. Campbell said, edging him away from the others. "Do you really think that heaven is porous, and that if we weren't so blind we would see many dead people among us?"

"Yes," he said, glancing at Nelson's family and professional advisers.

"I'm leaving tomorrow to spend some time with Monica in Naples," she said. "Could Nelson find me if it happens again?"

"I wouldn't worry about that," Spears replied. "This time he learned to let go."

A GRACIOUS VOICE

"I had the strangest dream last night," the Judge said. "I was riding a bicycle, and suddenly I was on a hill with tall, thin trees, like one of those old Indian burial mounds. When I tried to leave, the hill was surrounded with water up to my chest."

Harris Scintilton nodded as if he often spoke of dreams over lunch. Judge Swenson was expecting him to say something.

"What did you do with the bicycle?"

"It was Cynthia's bicycle, Harris. When I came up out of the water, I thought she was there someplace on the mound. Then I woke up."

Cynthia, Judge Swenson's daughter, had died of leukemia nearly thirty years earlier.

"When you called, I thought it was to help with

your campaign next year," the lawyer said slowly.

"There won't be another campaign. I'm starting chemotherapy next week."

Scintilton had seen many clients like this looking for some last encouragement.

"Then of·course there's hope."

"Only time, Harris. Maybe several months, a year at the outside."

"You'll stay on the bench?" Harris asked.

"Jane wants me to quit, but I can't, not yet," Judge Swenson said. "If I can stick it out until July, I'll have enough time in to retire on full pension. That's all I've got to leave her, Harris. She'll get my pension for life."

"You haven't told anyone?"

"Not the party, not the Governor," the Judge confided. "I don't want the jackals out stalking me while I'm still in my courtroom."

"If you want to come by the office, I'd be happy to help you with your estate plan," Harris volunteered.

The Judge smiled.

"I've been probate judge of this county for twenty-eight years. I've kept the records for all the marriages and deaths, and I can't even plan my own estate. Like everybody else, I have to go to a big law firm and pay big fees. I'm not asking for favors, Harris; I'll pay." Suddenly his hands were over his face. "God, my God, I'm going to die."

The lawyer glanced around. Most of the noon crowd at Barnie's was clustered at the bar, talking baseball and politics and what happened in court that morning. They knew enough to leave the Judge and his political advisor alone when they took the back booth.

"Listen, Harris. There's something I have to ask you."

Through the tears his eyes were pink. "Do you think we have to answer for our lives after we're dead?"

Scintilton studied him carefully to determine the answer he wanted to hear.

"Yes, Dwight, I think we do."

"Wagner's really screwed up on this one!" Douglas Frazier, senior trial attorney at Tenninger, Waylind & Tour, exclaimed as he, Harris Scintilton and Larry Tour reviewed the firm's accounts. "A damned contingency fee will contest, with $93,000 in unbilled fees and expenses and no end in sight."

"Now, Douglas, when he brought the Bracomb boys in here, they told a pretty good story, and it looked like an opportunity to do some work for the company, too," Tour said.

In his mid-forties, the son of the firm's founder had recently exchanged his pudgy wife and snarling teenaged sons for a succession of bright ties and high-pitched, frothy blonds.

"What a story," snorted Frazier. As a senior partner, he had reached the stage where he could criticize another lawyer's case, but no longer put together a good one himself. "The old man's nurse was giving him whole body massages, so he cut the boys out of his will and left nearly everything to her. Wagner's the only one around who'd believe it. Now three years, one will contest and $93,000 later, Anderson Page files a motion for summary judgment, and old Judge Swenson will probably throw the whole damn case out of court!"

Usually when Tour and Frazier started arguing about Allan Wagner at executive committee meetings, Scintilton stayed out of it. For about five years, Wagner had been Larry Tour's protégé, until he brought in several bad clients and got one of Tour's trusts in some major tax trouble. Now years of favoritism were turning into an embarrassment.

"You know, Larry, maybe I ought to get involved in the Bracomb will contest," Scintilton suggested softly. "Last thing in the world we need is Anderson Page boasting all over town how he nailed us in this one."

"Oh, thanks, Harris. I hadn't thought of that. Do you think there's some way to salvage it?" Tour asked eagerly.

"A will contest is a special statutory procedure. By law it has to go to a jury. The Judge will deny the motion for summary judgment."

"I read their motion," Frazier argued. "We just don't have a case."

"That's up to the jury," Scintilton replied. "Any case that goes to a jury has settlement value. What's the net estate?"

"Nine, close to ten million," Tour answered hopefully.

"A weak case means its settlement value is about a third, say three million five. We're on a one third contingency. We'll settle it for three to three-and-a-half million and take a fee of over a million dollars."

"You pull that off, and you can have my partnership share," snorted Frazier.

Looking at him intently, Scintilton did not reply. Frustrated that white hair and bushy eyebrows had not carried the argument, Frazier reached for something to preserve his position.

"But, Larry, this still doesn't resolve what we're going to do about Allan Wagner," he said.

"We can't just kick him out in the street," Tour snapped.

"Nothing like that, Larry," soothed Scintilton. "I just heard the probate judgeship is opening up soon. That might be just the place for someone who interned with us."

"Old Dwight Swenson is retiring?" Frazier exclaimed. "I don't believe it."

A contemporary of the probate judge, Douglas Frazier did not believe anyone should retire.

"Not retiring, Douglas. He's dying. And keep it to yourself, except when you call your friends in the Governor's office. Now, Larry, you know the key people on the Republican county committee. You should start making some calls about Allan, how he's just the man for the job if it ever opens up."

"How long do we have, Harris?" Tour asked eagerly.

"It will be out that he's sick in a few weeks, but he'll hide the diagnosis until July."

"That should be enough time," Frazier agreed. "How do we know Wagner will accept? Maybe he can't afford to go from two hundred thousand a year to ninety, or whatever a probate judge makes."

"Oh, he'll accept" Scintilton assured him. "It's either that or the street. Allan Wagner doesn't have anyplace else to go."

"Thanks for helping me out on this, Harris," Allan Wagner said eagerly.

Scintilton didn't respond. Apparently looking for something, he paged through the depositions in the Bracomb will contest.

"You know, Allan, you really ought to have the paralegals outline these. It's nearly impossible to keep track of all this without outlines."

"That's a good idea. I was thinking about doing that."

While his younger partner fidgeted, Scintilton read through the depositions for another half hour.

"Tell me about La Blaire Jackson, old man Bracomb's live-in cook," he finally said.

"Oh, she's one of the worst witnesses ever. Why, she didn't know anything about the old man and the nurse, even though she was his cook and housekeeper for seven years."

"Didn't you think that was strange?"

"Why, yes, but she gets $25,000 in the will herself. She's probably trying to protect that."

"Let me see those pictures of Bracomb again, "Scintilton said.

In the last summer of his life, Carl Bracomb had been photographed at a charity garden party, at the gala for the summer opera, and on his veranda overlooking the river.

"There's only one reason a man ninety-three would look that content," mused Scintilton.

"The nurse!" cried Wagner.

"How old is La Blaire Jackson? Here it is, in the deposition: twenty-six," Scintilton interrupted him.

"I don't know why you keep talking about the cook," complained Wagner. "After all, the will contest is about his nurse."

"That's the problem, isn't it, Allan? You don't have any evidence about the nurse. To the contrary, everyone you've deposed says she wasn't doing anything with the old man. She was engaged the year and a half she was there to a resident in sports medicine at University Hospital, and now she's married to him."

"You sound like Anderson Page," Wagner pouted.

"But the cook, Allan. There's your girl. On the premises the whole time, young, available, and too stupid to deny it effectively."

Allan Wagner just looked at him.

"But we don't have any evidence about her, either."

"The jury will think we do. And so will Anderson Page."

"Thanks, Harris, Allan. Thanks," repeated Judge Swenson, sitting back in the chair before Scintilton's desk. "You don't know how much better I feel with that done."

The two lawyers had just witnessed the Judge's new will and trust.

"And I really like the idea of putting the pension in the trust, to avoid probate with my major asset." Suddenly the Judge laughed. "Ironic, isn't it? The probate judge avoids probate."

"It is more private," Allan Wagner agreed, starting to repeat the discussion of an hour earlier.

"No one avoids probate ultimately," Scintilton said, shutting him off.

Judge Swenson blanched.

"Harris, there is something I'd like to talk to you about alone."

"Thanks, Allan," Scintilton said briskly to dismiss his junior partner.

With the look of a slow child who let a beach ball blow by without knowing whether he was supposed to catch it, Allan Wagner left the office.

"How's Wagner getting along?" the Judge inquired.

"Why do you ask?"

"Sometimes he doesn't seem to be too much on top of things."

"I'll be helping him out with the Bracomb will contest."

"Oh, well, then we can't discuss that. But Harris, really what I wanted to ask you, do you remember what you said when we had lunch, about being judged after we die?"

The Judge's eyes were pink; his face was strained.

"I've thought about it often," Harris answered softly.

"Do you think there's anything we can do now to prepare for that? I'm afraid, Harris. I'm so terribly afraid."

As if to assure himself the other man was ready to receive the answer, Scintilton studied him intently.

"We can make peace."

"What do you mean?" Judge Swenson asked eagerly, leaning forward.

"All those old cases on your docket, Dwight. Call the lawyers in and settle them."

"Do you really think that's what I should do?"

"Blessed are the peacemakers, for they shall be called sons of God," said Harris Scintilton.

"I've never seen old Dwight Swenson so anxious to settle a case," exclaimed Anderson Page as he, Scintilton, and Wagner left Judge Swenson's chambers, trailed by two of Page's associates.

"Sometimes he has a pretty good feel for things, Anderson. I don't think he wants to see your client cut out with nothing."

"Now, listen, Harris," Page bridled. "Your case is worth exactly $10,000, and that's what I've offered. If you have any kind of a feel for things, I'd suggest you and the Bracomb boys take it."

Behind Anderson Page, senior partner in Saloughby and Wales, his associates lifted their patrician heads to stare condescendingly at the lawyers from the rival firm.

"You didn't pick up on what he said about the trial time, did you?" Scintilton said, waving at the Judge's clerk and starting into the hall. Wagner hurried to keep up with his partner.

"One o'clock in the afternoon. Why, Harris?" Page called after him, fearing he had misunderstood something important. As if a case had been cited that they had missed, Page's associates glanced at each other nervously.

"Have you ever seen the jury pool in the afternoon, Anderson, after they've been picked over by the common pleas and municipal courts in the morning? There won't be any who haven't been kicked off a jury or two earlier in the day for cause or prejudice, or just plain stupidity."

"We have an airtight case, Scintilton," snapped Page.

Behind him his associates smiled knowingly at each other.

"With the jury you'll have, an airtight case is no better than fifty-fifty. That's why our demand for a third of the estate is so reasonable."

"Ten thousand, Scintilton, and not a dime more," Anderson Page cried after him.

Suddenly Harris Scintilton turned around.

"Then my offer of settlement is withdrawn."

Page's associates were as stunned as if the jury had just returned a verdict for the Bracomb brothers.

"Maybe you shouldn't have done that, Harris," Allan Wagner said, as they walked down the street to their office. "After all, $10,000 would pay for some of the depositions."

"We will settle for fifty per cent."

They walked another block in silence. To change the subject, Scintilton asked him if he thought he could ever be as strong a judge as Dwight Swenson.

"I've never thought much about that, Harris. Things are going along alright at the firm, aren't they?"

"You never know what might come along."

"Worst jury panel I've ever seen, Anderson," Scintilton said softly to the other lawyer as the jurors were led into the courtroom. "Know how to read those juror questionnaires? Look at Juror Number Seven. Thirty-six year old man married to an eighty-two year old woman. Want him deciding whether Mrs. Dr. Covington or the Bracomb boys get the money?"

Slapping the senior partner in Saloughby and Wales on the arm in a show of professional camaraderie, Scintilton returned to his own table. The eyes of Page's client and two associates followed him, then swept nervously over the prospective jurors until they rested on a man in a dirty T-shirt, with grease-stained green pants. Like a sleepy zoo creature looking dumbly through the bars who mistakes the smell of visitors for fish, Juror Number Seven caught the frightened stares and dropped his jaw.

"We have three peremptory challenges!" Page hissed across the courtroom.

"Mr. Page," snapped Judge Swenson. "I will have no exchanges among counsel."

Harris Scintilton smiled serenely at the ceiling. Jury selection in <u>Bracomb, et al vs Phyllis Marshal, Executrix. et al</u> had begun.

"Mr. Scintilton, you may inquire," the Judge intoned.

Almost languidly Harris Scintilton arose, strolled to the lectern and surveyed the prospective jurors. Several were staring at fixed points in the floor or ceiling; an overweight woman was trying to scratch some concealed spot by rotating in her chair; only Juror Number Seven acknowledged the lawyer's presence with a low, clucking sound. Taking a deep breath, the plaintiffs' counsel thought he smelled onion rings.

"The plaintiffs are satisfied, your honor. We pass for cause."

Only the lawyers and Phyllis Marshal, heiress pro temp, knew what that meant. It took Anderson Page a minute and a half to put his notes together to begin his inquiry, and two hours to show that none of the prospective jurors had gone beyond fifth grade, three had felony records they hadn't reported on their questionnaires, and none had the slightest understanding or concern for the world of the Bracombs, Phyllis Marshal, or sports medicine. By the time Page asked if they would be fair to all parties and follow the law given them by the Judge, those who were not comatose were whispering among themselves, trying to find the onion rings.

At three-thirty, just as the maintenance staff turned off the air conditioning for the day, Judge Swenson sustained Page's challenges for cause to the three felons. A woman was excused for an operation the next morning, and a young man with long, dirty hair was excused to begin serving a sentence for a traffic offense.

"No more challenges for cause," Judge Swenson told Anderson Page at the side bar. "Let's get moving."

After Page had used up his three peremptory challenges, the onion rings left the courtroom, but Juror Number Seven, the thirty-six year old man with the eighty-two year old wife, was still working his jaw at Phyllis Marshal. By four, when the deputies started locking the courthouse doors, the jury had been impaneled and excused until one the next afternoon.

"Looks like your client has another admirer," Scintilton remarked to opposing counsel as he and Wagner started out of the courtroom.

"Look, Harris, what do you know about this half day business?" Page started after him. "The Judge isn't drinking or anything, is he?"

"Just trying to keep his paperwork under control." Scintilton paused, so that Page's client and associates would be close enough to overhear. "And I wouldn't say things like that about him in this courtroom, Anderson. It just might get you held in contempt."

Anderson Page's cross examinations of the Bracomb brothers rivaled Perry Mason, and would have held even the most jaded viewer of *L.A. Law* spellbound on the couch. By question, gesture, document, and intonation, the lawyer demonstrated the years of alcoholism, drug abuse, profligacy, and neglect that had led Carl Bracomb to disinherit his sons in favor of his female attendant. When the younger Bracomb protested his filial devotion, Page countered that it was his own attempt on Miss Marshal's virtue that had led to the final rupture.

"He's killing us," Allan Wagner whispered to Scintilton.

"Not with this jury. They think young Richard is some kind of hero."

Scintilton exaggerated: most of the jurors were staring at the floor or the ceiling One juror, who apparently could tell time, was looking at the clock at the back of the room. Only Juror Number Seven had listened to the witness, bobbing his head with every sneering answer.

"Well done, Anderson," Scintilton smiled as he rose to redirect his client. "Couldn't have elicited that much sympathy if I'd tried."

Page snorted, his associates curled their lips, and his client blinked nervously. Sharply, venomously, Page objected to nearly every question, hamstringing Scintilton's attempt to rehabilitate his client. At each rebuff Scintilton looked hurt and abused, and Richard Bracomb appeared more and more terrified as he saw a lifetime of inherited leisure slipping away from him. Returning to his seat, head down, Scintilton smiled again at Page.

"Thanks, Anderson. Look at that jury."

Stunned, bewildered, Juror Number Seven was working his lips, as if he had put too many pieces of bubblegum in his mouth at once.

Following the mid afternoon recess, Scintilton called La Blaire Jackson to the stand. After identifying her as Carl Bracomb's cook and the recipient of $25,000 in his will, Scintilton asked: "What did you do to earn it?"

It took La Blaire Jackson a minute and a half to repeat she was a cook. While she stuttered, Scintilton glanced at Phyllis Marshal, the erstwhile heiress. Hardly breathing, she had crumpled a piece of paper on the table.

"That wasn't all, was it?" Harris continued.

Frantically the cook looked around the courtroom for help. On one side the jury, with Juror Number Seven licking his lower lip; above her Judge Swenson, as pale as old Bracomb after his third stroke; on the other side Miss Marshal, tightening the wad of paper in her fist.

"Let me help you, Miss Jackson. Do you know what fellatio is?" Scintilton asked solicitously.

Again the anguished stare.

"Would it help if I described it?"

"I object!" cried Anderson Page.

"Overruled. He may cross examine a beneficiary as an opposing party," ruled the Judge.

In exquisite detail Scintilton described the act.

"Am I refreshing your recollection, Miss Jackson?"

Her eyes met the eyes of Juror Number Seven, and she recoiled.

"Was that a nod?" demanded Scintilton, catching her movement. "We need a verbal answer for the record."

"Yes," said Miss Jackson, agreeing they needed a verbal answer.

"You bitch!" screamed Phyllis Marshal. "I told you to leave him alone!"

"All I ever brought him at night was milk and cookies," Miss Jackson sobbed. "It was you with those red pills and white powder that killed him."

"I won't have it!" cried Judge Swenson. "Gentlemen! Mr. Page! Another outburst like this and I'll hold your client in contempt!"

"Your honor," sputtered Page.

"We'll take a fifteen minute recess. I want to see counsel in chambers. In five minutes!" the Judge croaked.

As the jury lurched out, Page and his associates surrounded their client, breaking the deadly gaze of the witness. Chin tight, eyes hard, La Blaire Jackson held her place in the witness chair, as proud as Cassandra before the elders of Troy.

"You tricked her, Harris. You tricked her!" hissed Wagner.

Clenching his jaw Scintilton stared at the counsel table.

"How can you just sit there like that? What are you thinking?" demanded Alan Wagner.

"I'm beginning to wish we had a better jury," replied Harris Scintilton.

As the lawyers entered the Judge's chambers, the building air conditioning was going off. Warm, metallic air from the old pipes mixed with the sharper smell of fresh vomit from the Judge's bathroom. Without his robe and suit jacket, Judge Swenson was an old man in a sweat stained white shirt, shaking with sickness and anger.

"Gentlemen, in twenty-eight years on the bench, I have never seen such an outrage. I am thinking very seriously of holding your client in contempt, Mr. Page."

"Your honor, if the Court would understand," Page began.

"And why this case hasn't been settled, I'll never know. With what we just heard and this jury, neither of you has better than a fifty-fifty chance."

"We've been trying to settle this all along, your honor," Scintilton said softly.

"Then why don't you do it? Come on, now, Harris, what's your demand? One third, wasn't it?"

"We had to withdraw that before trial, Judge. Now we're at fifty-percent of the net estate."

Anderson Page's eyes narrowed, and his associates drew back in disbelief.

"Well?" the Judge snapped at Page.

"That's outrageous! When I get Miss Jackson on direct, she can explain everything."

"Will you talk to your client?" demanded the Judge.

Stunned, Page's lips worked around unformed, unspoken words.

"I'll talk to her."

For ten minutes, Scintilton and Wagner sat silently with the Judge, listening to far away bangs in the air conditioning system as the pipes slowly warmed.

"Damned hot for June," the Judge finally said.

"Wouldn't want to be here in July," Scintilton agreed.

Then the door opened and Anderson Page returned without his associates to say that his client would accept the Bracombs' settlement demand.

"Harris, there's something I want to say to you," Allan Wagner said as the two lawyers walked back to their office from the courthouse.

Expecting a compliment, Scintilton smiled fondly at his junior partner. Had he finally recognized the difference between a fee of $10,000 and a third of five million? $5,000,000?

"Yes, Allan?"

"You were asking the other day about what I'd do if I were a judge?"

"Yes?"

"I'd never let a lawyer get away with what you just pulled, Harris. Never."

For the first time, Scintilton saw character and command in the younger man's face.

"Let's worry about that when it happens," Harris replied.

"It's a hell of a settlement, Harris," Douglas Frazier applauded his partner as the executive committee of Tenninger, Waylind & Tour completed its review of the Bracomb will contest.

"With this fee we can carry Allan Wagner for a few more years" Scintilton suggested.

"You can forget that, Harris. He's history," Tour said.

"But he showed a new quality at the trial, " Scintilton argued. "I don't think we should let him get away from us so soon."

"What are you talking about? If you hadn't taken over the case, he would have lost it!" Frazier exclaimed.

The lawyer paused; how could he tell his partners that what Allan Wagner had showed at the trial was integrity?

"He needs more experience with us before he goes on the bench," Harris insisted.

"Not a chance now," Larry Tour interjected. "We've already called in all our chips with the local party and in the state capitol. Allan Wagner will be out next probate judge."

"It's a done deal," Frazer concluded. "We'd look like perfect fools if we tried to back out of it now."

Scintilton was stunned; he had always been able to sway his partners with a big fee.

"I just don't think he's ready."

"Shouldn't bother you, Harris. After all, he learned everything he knows from you, didn't he?" Frazier said to comfort him.

Scintilton wanted to say that Wagner could change the whole system, from how they computed legal fees to requiring the estate be closed before paying the lawyers. But he knew his partners well enough to see he was beaten.

"I guess you're right, Douglas," Larry Tour smiled. "With his share of our fee in the Bracomb case, he'll be able to pay for his own campaign next year. I'm sure he wouldn't feel right about asking his former partners for money."

"I hadn't thought of that at all," muttered Harris Scintilton.

MEMORIES OF A
FAMILY VACATION

I didn't want to go to the lake again; it was Lillian's idea; her family has a place beside the bay. For them it held wonderful memories: how their grandfather won it in a poker game; the drives up from Chicago in the forties and fifties; freighters passing through the sinking sun on the horizon. For me it brought flashbacks to our honeymoon, a hellish week when the septic tank overflowed daily, and we only had Lillian's cooking to tide us through. Worst were her father's monologues about the Second World War, where he acted out his hatred for the human race as second in command of a destroyer.

Night after night, inflamed by bourbon and darkness, he gathered the family around him on the huge porch overlooking the bay. As children yawned and adults reached for another drink, he told how they caught the submarine on the surface near the Carolina coast in early 1942. They holed the conning tower with first shot, and as they turned for another firing run, their searchlight caught the terrified Germans pouring out the hatches and diving into the sea.

In the second before the Captain could order them to slow to pick up the survivors, Lillian's father shouted, "Away depth charges!"

"The Captain was a sucker for a sob story," the old man snickered. "Should have seen those Nazi bastards' faces when they saw what I'd done."

Screaming, the Germans tried to swim out of the way in the seconds before the depth charges exploded. Then the sea erupted around them like boils, killing them all from concussion. The destroyer slowed, and they hauled the bodies aboard with boat hooks.

"Looked like they were sleeping," he always said softly at the end to create a sense of complicity with his listeners.

After being stripped of their uniforms and any body parts that might interest weapons designers, they were buried in an under utilized government cemetery on Nags Head. I had to listen to that story for two weeks every summer for thirty-five years. When he finally died, I looked forward to the silence as much as to Lillian's inheritance. I was disappointed in both.

All the years I served as counsel for the down state factories, Lillian's brother Tom prowled the Chicago headquarters, insinuating himself into every facet of the company. From file clerk to director, they all owed their jobs to Tom. Not until the old man died did we learn that Tom had recapitalized the company. He inherited all the voting stock; Lillian and her sister Louise were left with non-voting stock that paid a meager dividend and effectively excluded their husbands from management.

Along with Louise's husband Harold, I accepted Tom's grinning offer of early retirement. At the least the dividend would keep up with Lillian's credit card bills, and I could concentrate on my Civil War stamp collection. Louise and Harold checked into an upscale detoxification center in West Palm Beach, never to return to the lake.

Instead of a life of quiet detachment, however, Lillian insisted on recreating the family holidays of her childhood, with Tom filling in for her father, and his wife Virginia for Louise. They looked like sisters, with the same boney knees, layered blond hair and spa-enhanced tans. Tom relished his role, too, always arriving late on the company jet, with breathless new stories of his most recent encounters on the Republican National Committee or the Defense Policy Board. Six figure contributions gained him easy access to politicians and government purchasing agents; a million dollars earned him and Virginia a night on cots in the tack room at Bush's Crawford ranch.

"Laura said it was the first time anyone besides family stayed there," Virginia confided.

So now, as the sun sank over Lake Michigan, we heard another bourbon-steeped voice bragging of business coups and newly commissioned projects from the Department of Defense. Instead of stories about dead Germans in the surf, we heard how the administration savaged the congressional Democrats. In place of the indecisive destroyer captain, we had Donald Rumsfeld secretly funding incredible new weapons systems for which Tom's company was the prime contractor. As the ice melted and the shadows lengthened, I found myself reaching for the bottle again, just as I had when the old man sat in the oversize wicker chair with the moldy cushions.

"It's supposed to rain tomorrow," Lillian said as she turned out the bedroom light. "Virginia and I are going to Charlevoix to shop."

Good, I thought. Bad roads, too many tourists, thunderstorms - maybe there'll be an accident.

"Will Tom be going?" I asked hopefully.

"Weren't you listening when he said he has to fly to Washington for a meeting with Mr. Rumsfeld?"

So if fortune struck, it would only be the two of them. Not perfect but still not a bad thought to end the day. And Tom would be gone for the weekend. If I had learned anything from Lillian's father, it was that good bourbon could ease the mind.

But not that night. The storm came early with a flash through the curtains and a sharp thunder crack. The wind was up, moaning over the bay like drowning men. Before the rain swept in, there was a series of thumps! from the water, rhythmic and erratic like a child pounding on blocks. Then the wind suddenly died. I lay in the air conditioning waiting for the storm, while Lillian snored beside me. Except for a few more flashes like searchlights sweeping the house, nothing happened. I had to go to the bathroom twice before I could get back to sleep.

I was always the first one up. The kitchen faced the road, and while the coffee was brewing I would walk up to the mailbox for the paper. Then I would pour my coffee, go out to the porch and sit down in the big wicker chair. As usual Tom hadn't bothered to put the bourbon away. I was scanning the headlines, hoping for something better than another California murder, when I saw the submarine.

It was lying on its side about a hundred yards out, gently rocking in the surf, a hole punched in the conning tower. Pieces of black cloth bobbed about it drifting toward the shore. I opened the screen door for a better look. Those weren't pieces of cloth; those were bodies, some of them already bloated and splitting the black uniforms. I ran down to the beach.

Have you ever seen a dead man in the water newly drowned? Barely out of his teens, his blond hair floated gently in the little waves and his eyes were tight shut, as if he had tried to stave off death with darkness. The backs of his fingers brushed the sand. For a moment I just stood watching the water wash in and out of his hands.

His uniform still fit perfectly. The only ornament was an eagle over his heart clutching a swastika in its talons. I looked out at the wreck again. There was a beautiful red seahorse painted on the conning tower just in front of the hole. Then another body touched the shore, this one not so beautiful. The right arm and shoulder were gone, leaving a deep red opening for minnows to explore.

I ran back to the house. Tom was in the kitchen reading something from his wallet into his cell phone.

"Tom!" I cried.

He shushed me with a gesture.

"I've got Rummy on hold," he whispered fiercely.

"Yes, that's right," he said into the phone. "Now read the account number back. OK. You got it. Thanks."

He hit another button.

"Don? Sorry. You wouldn't believe what I have to deal with here. Okay. Ten-thirty. On my way."

"Tom, I .."

"It's all taken care of. I'll call tonight."

He was out the door and into the BMW before I could ask what had happened. Was somebody filming a movie and there had been a terrible accident? In ten minutes Tom's jet would be circling south over the bay. I went back to the porch. The submarine had heeled over on its side, spilling more bodies out the hatches.

The first ambulance was driving up the beach when Lillian called from the kitchen.

"We're going now, dear."

How was I going to explain it to them? I went back to the kitchen.

"Oh, you needn't have come," she said. "We've decided to have breakfast in town."

Normally that would have been good news; breakfast was not one of her good meals.

"You look terrible," she said. "Is something the matter?"

I glanced at Virginia. Her face expressed a horror that monthly Botox injections could not suppress. Had she looked out their bedroom window and seen what was lying in the surf?

"I talked to Tom," I began.

"Let's go," Virginia snapped. "I'm hungry."

They were gone before I could tell them what Tom had said. I made another pot of coffee and went back to the porch.

It was the longest day of my life. All morning the ambulances drove in along the beach, huge red crosses in white circles on the sides of the brown trucks. I wondered why they didn't use the new Humvees, but they were probably all in Iraq. Soldiers in puttees waded out into the surf and pulled the bodies to the shore. One by one, they lifted them onto stretchers and loaded them into the ambulances.

The tugs didn't arrive until mid afternoon. Men in wet suits climbed aboard the submarine and secured it with lines to the tugs. Then the boats moved back and forth, white wakes roiling the turquoise water, until they had worked the submarine off the sandbar. Suddenly the conning tower swung upright, dropping a last body into the lake. Soldiers from the ambulance waded out for it. I saw the boat for the last time when I came back from the kitchen with a glass of ice. As the tugs towed it out into the bay, the ugly gray bow, notched with torpedo tubes, pointed at the shore.

Strengthened by the whisky, I thought maybe it wasn't such a bad thing to depth charge the bastards after all.

"You started without us," Lillian said, sweeping onto the porch in a rush of paper bags and gift shop smells. "We've had such a wonderful day, haven't we, Ginny?"

"I'm going upstairs to change," Virginia called from the dining room.

"We're going to the Busy Bee for dinner," Lillian announced. "Now look what I bought."

So I emitted little grunts at Lillian's latest designer acquisitions, as the ice melted and the glass turned warm in my hand. By the time the last package was opened, the lake was as vacant as it was every other evening. Even the truck tracks in the sand had disappeared, washed over by the little tide. Then Virginia called from the kitchen that she was ready, and Lillian drove us into town. I was glad I had not had another drink at the house. It was better to save my allotment for dinner, when they would recap the day's bargains like hunters recounting a good kill.

It was still light when we returned to the house. Lillian and Virginia said they were going to the porch to watch the sunset.

"I think I'll take a walk," I said.

"Be careful," my wife said without much conviction.

"I'm just going along the beach."

Instead I walked along the dunes. For a few moments every day, as the sky lost its color, you could wonder if we really were alone in the universe, and whether our dreams were our own.

"Hey, Buddy!" a voice called from a dark space between the dunes. "Is there anyplace around here a fella can get something to eat?"

I was so surprised I could hardly breath. He stepped up beside me on the dune, a seersucker jacket over his arm.

In his early thirties, he had a broad forehead and dark blond hair combed straight back. Too pale to be a vacationer, he looked like a lawyer up from Chicago for the weekend.

"We just had dinner down the road," I said. "Where did you park?"

He was as startled as I was when he first called.

"I'll have to walk."

There was an echo in his voice, as if he had to form each word in his mind before he uttered it.

"It's a beautiful evening," he said, looking out at the lake like a bad actor trying to be convincing.

I glanced at his feet. I hadn't seen two-tone shoes like that since I was a kid.

"How about a smoke?" he asked, taking a silver cigarette case out of his jacket.

"I don't smoke."

"Well, thanks, Buddy," he said holding out his hand.

It was wet with sweat.

"Do you have any luggage?" I asked. "I could get the car."

"No need to trouble yourself. See you around."

He returned quickly to the dark place. I had never seen anyone so afraid in my life.

Lillian had left the kitchen door open and the back porch light off. I was opening the refrigerator for some ice when someone knocked on the screen. Maybe the lawyer had decided to take me up on the ride after all. I turned on the light and went to the door. Two men in double-breasted suits and straw hats were standing under the yellow light.

"I guess you know why we're here," the bigger one said, holding up a wallet with a FBI badge.

"I was wondering when somebody would come," I began. "Tom said he'd talk to Rumsfeld and would call, but I haven't heard anything.

The big man looked at his companion. The smaller man took out a package of Lucky Strikes and offered one to the speaker. Then he lighted their cigarettes with a Zippo.

"I don't know about any Rumsfeld," the big man said slowly. "But I do know we found a raft out on the dunes. Looked like somebody tried to bury it."

My chest tightened so hard I couldn't speak. The smaller man stepped forward and pointed at me with his cigarette.

"We figure the submarine came in to land a spy. Just luck that destroyer caught them."

What had I read they did with the German saboteurs they caught during the War? Tried them before military tribunals and electrocuted them the next day with J. Edgar Hoover watching through the sweating glass.

"Yes, Sir," I choked out.

"Nothing for you to be afraid of," the big man said. "Just call our office if you see anything funny."

He held out his card. I could be a hero, maybe get an award from the Department of Defense, or I could give a terrified man a few more hours alone.

"I can find the number in the book," I said.

"Suit yourself," the big man said.

I turned off the porch light and listened to them drive away.

"Is that you?" Lillian called from the porch.

I picked up my glass and joined them. They had left the big wicker chair for me. I sat down and poured myself a drink.

"Tom said he'd call," I began.

"That's none of your business," Virginia snapped and stalked inside.

I just looked at Lillian.

"You have to be more sensitive," she said. "She had a terrible fight with Tom last night about her credit cards. He had to call the bank this morning to straighten it out."

"I wasn't talking about credit cards."

"Oh. I'll try to talk to her then."

She stood up.

"But you do have to be more sensitive."

So now I am alone on the big family porch, as the last Monet colors drain from the sky. Maybe the Department of Defense is experimenting with time travel, so our military can outflank the enemy in the fourth dimension. Maybe something went terribly wrong, or Tom told them this was the perfect place for an experiment. How long do experiments take? What about the FBI and the man on the dunes? If I saw a man on an airplane lighting his shoe, I'd tell someone, I think. But I didn't tell them tonight.

If I am prosecuted, I will defend by asking what damage a Nazi saboteur could do sixty years too late? But who could have imagined what a few men with box cutters could do, if they took over an airplane? I will say that I panicked and didn't know what to say. Could I even get my own lawyer to believe me?

I have been too long on this porch. Old houses absorb odors; I smelled Lillian's mother's perfume in the living room last week. Perhaps they absorb memories, too, releasing them when a susceptible person passes through a familiar room. I should go to bed, but Tom did promise to call.

I am almost anxious for him to return.

THE HISTORIAN

An odd event during the reign of the Emperor Tiberius may explain everything. While touring the Middle East, Germanicus, the wildly popular grandson of Augustus Caesar fell ill in Antioch. Necromancy was suspected. Germanicus tore up the floor of his villa and found a dead baby and lead tablets in the Chaldean language invoking unknown gods for his death. Despite every precaution, the young prince worsened and died. Piso, Proconsul of Syria, was recalled to Rome and accused of poisoning him, but the trial ended abruptly when Piso was found in his bath with the doors locked from the inside and his throat cut.

Louise and I lived in a New York style apartment building, twenty stories of blackened brick with classical pediments around the windows and a portico at the entrance wide enough for two Cadillacs abreast. Two generations before us, the Bellevedere had stood at the entrance to the city's most prosperous neighborhood. After an initial influx of spinsters, widows and bachelor uncles washed through in the twenties and early thirties, however, the building became the haunt of retired couples, single schoolteachers, and an occasional academic homesick for the East Coast. Sitting beside their Rookwood fireplaces, they could look out over the synagogue and delicatessens and imagine they were in Manhattan or Boston and that the streetcars had destinations like Fifth Avenue or Cambridge.

The neighborhood changed so slowly that nobody really noticed until the riots in the sixties, just before I moved in. On the fire-blackened morning when the exhausted looters finally withdrew, the retirees peered out over the debris of an American Kristallnacht and departed for their children's' houses in the suburbs. I was able to lease a two-bedroom apartment for half the regular rent, becoming the first non-tenured faculty member from City University to reside at the Bellevedere.

I seduced Louise there, or she seduced me. She had thick auburn hair that always smelled clean and a figure that seemed so anxious for release when I undressed her. Sometimes I wondered what attracted her to me, a thin, black haired historian with thick glasses who still wore his college graduation suit.

"It's your mind," she would say, laughing.

We met when I was a teaching assistant for the professor giving her senior seminar. She made me think that my remarks on the intrigues in the Emperor Augustus' household were as clever and stimulating as the sitcoms to which she compared them. Our first night as a married couple, we laughed about the thumping steam heat, the clanking pipes, and the occasional rustle of rodents between the floors.

"Do you ever wonder how many people have died in this room?" she asked as we lay on the damp sheets.

Not wanting to think about death, I just touched her hand.

"Or in this building?" she continued.

I didn't care, and when I turned to her again she laughed as if she didn't care, either.

We were so young, and everything was still an adventure. Looking out over the avenue, we rejoiced as carryouts and Laundromats opened in the shells of the delicatessens and florist shops. Surely the neighborhood will revive, we thought, when Don Wong's Chinese Restaurant replaced the abandoned shoe repair shop on the corner.

One festival Sunday we even attended Mt. Zion Baptist Church, which had moved into the synagogue after the congregation had emigrated beyond the beltway. Had we walked around the block from the Bellevedere, we would have seen the "for sale" signs marking the neighborhood's death. But I was an historian, and historians look back, not around. If they notice anything about their surroundings, it is some allusion to the past, never a portent for what is to come.

Our first two years at the Bellevedere, I was working on my thesis on Tacitus' *Histories* and Louise was hoping for children; then I was writing the text that would earn me tenure. After learning that there would be no children, Louise began her thesis on the role of aristocratic widows as regents in the Midi during the ninth and tenth centuries. Due to the difficulty finding source material, she was frequently absent.

Sometimes we would meet for a week or ten days between quarters or a summer in Provence; sometimes I passed the entire winter alone, grading papers in the extra bedroom and listening to the windows shudder in the cold. On one summer adventure, Louise confided that in the ninth century, widows were protected by the souls of their dead husbands, who could not enter the realm of the dead until their heirs were enthroned. At my suggestion, she confined this legend to a footnote.

When she returned the last time from Carcassonne, she hung a basket of artificial flowers on the wall outside our door. To distinguish the seasons she put out corncobs and dried flowers in the fall, a Santa with a white cotton beard at Christmas, and a bouquet of plastic tulips mixed with lilies of the valley in the spring.

After Louise had defended her thesis, she found a feminist publisher. Then she left me for book tours. She returned jet lagged and exhilarated, unable to sleep for nights. Staring into the dark, she wondered whether there was any meaning in settling cracks, and why the leaves brushed the window at just such a time.

"Listen, Walter," she would say, awakening me in the night. "Do you hear something rustling?"

"Just the leaves," I said.

"It could be Dr. Martin's soul trying to find a memory he left behind when he died," she whispered, squeezing my fingers.

Dr. Martin had lived in our apartment from the mid-thirties until 1957. One afternoon, when I was rearranging the books beside the fireplace, one of the shelves collapsed. Stuck to the wall was a yellowing newspaper photograph of Dr. Martin at his retirement party sipping punch from a crystal cup.

Although Louise and I were both on the history faculty, we pursued different academic tracks. I passed the years taking careful notes on three by five cards, publishing my *Remembrances of Imperial Rome* and *Intrigues of the Later Caesars,* and writing new introductions for the histories of deceased scholars, so my publisher could keep them in print. I attended faculty conferences, sat on thesis panels and even lectured occasionally at a major university. Louise diverted from feminist studies into architectural history, particularly apartments built between 1900 and 1930, and something she called "the winnowing process."

"After people die," she confided one night, "they stay around sifting their memories, deciding which to keep and which to discard. You can never be free if you are imprisoned by memory."

"Like an historian," I said.

"The process takes years, sometimes decades. In buildings like this, it is going on all the time."

"What if they want to stay the same?" I wondered.

"Then they are damned," she said sharply. "We are not judged by what we do but by what we remember."

When I looked at her, she turned away and curled up. That night something was scratching behind the baseboard. I wondered what could be so attractive about old wood, unless it was the smell of death.

Winnowing Memories was the book that brought her a new publisher plus an introduction to countless mediums and investigators of paranormal phenomena. When the department would not give her leave for another book tour, she resigned her lectureship. Her next books on feminism and the paranormal were wildly successful. Her circle was in Los Angeles; sometimes I thought she came back to be with the Bellevedere more than to be with me. When she thought I was asleep, I could hear her whispering to the rustling walls and laughing when the leaves brushed the window.

I suppose we were happy in a way. Then Louise began to grow old. She forgot to put up the Santa after Thanksgiving. That was the year they started talking about my retirement at our department meetings. Apparently I was being criticized for being late to lectures. They never should have allowed students to rate the faculty. How could I answer anonymous accusations about drifting from subject to subject during seminars and occasionally wandering out of the classroom altogether?

"I am still working on my essay on the fragments of Archilochus," I told the chairman. "It will be a proud day for the department when it is published."

I am sure I had other recent accomplishments, but after so much time, it is difficult to find anything that distinguishes one year from the others. You may as well mark the days by the daily specials at Don Wong's Chinese Restaurant.

When I came home that evening with a double order of Kung Pao chicken, Louise was weeping. Someone in the department must have called her, I thought. But no; she was holding an envelope from the building management. They were converting the Bellevedere into condominiums. We had six months to decide whether to purchase our unit or move elsewhere.

"Of course we'll buy it," I reassured her. "Everything will be exactly as it has always been."

"You don't understand," she sniffed. "A condominium is like a pre-planned funeral. It means we have roots. My God, Walter, why can't we still be young?"

We had never had a mortgage. It made us feel so free.

"Aren't you tired of being tired all the time?" she continued.

I wasn't tired all the time, and when I was, it gave me a good reason not to do anything I didn't want to do.

"Maybe you should see a doctor," I suggested.

"I can't stand the pretense," she said. "The most they can do is keep you from dying quite so soon."

When the papers came from the developer, I signed them. Louise returned reinvigorated from her lecture in Vermont, and we celebrated our purchase with a split of champagne at the faculty club. When she returned to our table from the bathroom, she was pressing her side, as if something she didn't understand was tugging at her. That night she told me she wasn't sure we had done the right thing.

"There's hardly anyone left to talk to anymore," she said.

All our old neighbors had died or moved to assisted living.

"I'm here," I protested.

"I'm not talking about you, Walter. Dr. Martin finally decided what to do about his memories of medical school. Now there's only Betty Klosterman on six and Mort Gottlieb on fifteen trying to make up their minds about their affair."

"It has been a long time since anybody died here," I agreed.

"It's the young people," she said. "Everyone here is so damned young."

I remembered that I did occasionally see a young couple entering or leaving the apartment next door. Sometimes I even heard music through the wall when I walked to the elevator.

After the conversion to condominiums, the noises at the Bellevedere changed. Now we heard hammering and nighttime clanks as do-it-your-selfers reconfigured spaces unchanged for sixty years and tried to remodel bathrooms without a plumber.

"I'm not feeling well," Louise said after such a night. "I haven't been able to sleep."

She was lying on her back pressing her side.

"Maybe you should reschedule the Santa Barbara seminar," I suggested.

"I'll stay in bed today."

Her beautiful hair was thick and damp, as if she had not washed it for a long time.

I made her tea and toast. As I was eating the toast for dinner, the telephone rang. I had missed a faculty meeting. The chairman was very angry.

"It's Louise," I explained. "She isn't well, you know."

"Oh," he said. "I'm sorry. I didn't know."

Everyone was very understanding, even the people in Santa Barbara. They called to ask if she had missed her plane.

"Isn't she there?" I asked. "She said she was going."

"Do you think something happened to her?" the female voice said with some alarm.

"I'm sure if something were wrong, she would call," I explained.

So Louise just lay in bed and talked about her memories.

"Do you remember the first time we made love?" she asked. "Do you remember the shoe repair shop next to the Laundromat before the Chinese restaurant? What do you remember?"

"I am working on Archilochus. Everything is flux."

"We have to winnow our memories, Walter, or they will drag us down."

That was when I moved into the extra bedroom. When we were much younger, we thought that we might have a visitor. It was very convenient now. Couples in long relationships need to be able to get away from each other.

The last time I went to the university, they were having a retirement party for me. Everyone was sorry that Louise was out of town.

"We left a voice mail for her to come," one of the graduate students said.

"She travels a lot," I explained.

I didn't want to admit that I didn't know how to work the voice mail.

"Do you remember when you were a teaching assistant for Professor Langston?" Louise asked when I returned. "Should I keep that one?"

"I wish you would," I replied.

"I'm not sure," she said. "You always looked away when I tried to catch your eye."

"You would be a different person if you didn't remember me," I said.

"Oh, yes," she agreed.

One afternoon, when I was getting off the elevator with my groceries, the young couple down the hall approached me.

"Hi," she said. "I'm Tina. This is Sean. We thought maybe you needed some help with the condo."

She was hardly old enough to be a graduate student.

"Everything's fine," I replied. "Why do you ask?"

"There's been a funny smell," she said.

"Sometimes I forget the garbage. I eat a lot of Chinese food."

"We could remind you," Tina suggested.

"Yes. That would be nice."

A few days later, as I was talking with Louise about her memories of the summer of 1967, someone knocked on the door. We were both startled.

"I don't want any company," Louise said.

It was the young couple, each with a handful of large plastic bags. They were very helpful. I hadn't realized how many old carryout containers I had stacked in the kitchen and living room.

"Maybe you should open a window," Tina suggested, looking at the closed bedroom door. "It's, well, stuffy in here."

"They're painted shut," I said.

"Sean will help, won't you, Sean?"

"Sure thing," Sean said.

Looking at them, I wondered if they had ever worn anything besides jeans and tennis shoes. At least they could relate to their students. They both taught in the anthropology department.

"I can't let them see me like this," Louise said when I told her how they would come the next week to help clean up her room.

She really wasn't much fun anymore, only talking about what she remembered and unwilling to meet new people. So I thought of a way to make her and my young neighbors happy. I went next door and borrowed Sean's hammer and crow bar.

"Can I help?" he asked.

"It's just a loose floorboard," I explained. "I can handle it."

Louise was mumbling about her memories of Provence as I lifted her out of bed. The blanket caught under the mattress, and when I jerked it loose, something dropped to the floor on the far side of the bed. She had lost so much weight it was easy to carry her into the living room.

It was harder for me to pull aside the area rug than to pry up the floorboards. What surprised me was how little space there was. I unwrapped Louise and laid her between the joists.

"How's that?" I asked as I tucked her in.

She didn't say anything. Then I discovered that the floorboards wouldn't lie flat. While I was pressing on them, somebody knocked at the door.

"Need any help?" Sean called.

"I'm nearly finished," I replied. "See you on garbage night."

I flopped the area rug over the raised floorboards. To avoid tripping on the hump, I placed the butler's tray table over it. Two nights later she finally stopped talking about her memories. Peace at last, I thought, until Sean and Tina came on garbage night. I really should have cleaned up Louise's room myself and presented them with a row of anonymous garbage bags.

"My God!" Sean cried from the bedroom. "It's a foot!"

"Just talk to him," Tina said. "I'll call someone."

So Sean and I sat in the kitchen while I ate my Kung Pao chicken and talked about my early work on Tacitus. At first it was an ordinary conversation; he seemed very interested. Then I heard someone moving furniture in the living room.

"I wonder how long it's been here," a male voice said.

Tina must have called a lot of people. Ambulance attendants, someone from the coroner's office, even the pastor of Mt. Zion Baptist Church stopped by. Finally two police officers joined us.

"Professor," one of them said, fidgeting with his cap. "Can you tell us how a body got under the floor boards in your living room?"

Sean looked at me as if I should know.

"An odd event during the reign of the Emperor Tiberius may explain everything," I began.

Sean nodded, and the police took careful notes.

After I said goodbye to Sean and Tina, the officers drove me to University Hospital. It was becoming difficult to separate what I remembered from what Louise wanted to forget. So I haven't been very clear when I talk to people about my case. Apparently they decided that something bad had happened. I had to move to a big brick building with a chain link fence around it in a dark part of the city.

Now I live in a light green room with a cot, a chair, a toilet and a radio, and eat macaroni several times a week. I read without remembering to pass the days. Sean and Tina came to visit me once. They brought Kung Pao chicken. We talked about the mysterious death of Piso, once proud Proconsul of Syria.

Perhaps Louise was right about winnowing our memories. We are what we forget. Monuments crumble, papyrus withers, and all my histories fade. How can I preserve my life? I shall copy the history of everything into a huge computer and bury it in a mountain beneath tons of radioactive waste, where no one will ever disturb it. Silicon never forgets. But if no one accesses the hard drive, it may as well be scrubbed as clean as a stele washed smooth by the rain. Trees fall and no one hears them; so do empires; so will I. History is an undersea mountain in the path of the blind submarine, waiting to destroy. Memory is impossible. I shall tell that to Louise the next time she whispers to me.

EMBRACING THE
INNER CHILD

The subconscious is a child, and like an angry child must be kept locked in its room. When I entered *Lillian's Wine Bar* that evening, I wasn't looking for my inner child; I was looking for Judy Revak, who had promised me a shot at her real estate agency's virtual tour business. *Lillian's* is a place where middle aged realtors, car salespeople, and insurance types gather in turtle necked comfort to drink Merlot, celebrate an occasional sale, and bemoan missed quotas and alimony payments.

My glasses fogged up, so I waited in a rain forest of cologne and hair spray for Judy's "Oh, my God!" voice, hoping Barry Hartman wasn't there. Hartman just wouldn't let go of my video of a foot sticking out the bathroom door on one of my first shoots.

"Was it Harry or Sally in there?" he'd call so everyone would hear, and he could tell the story again. "Lucky they didn't have you do the bedroom!"

When my glasses cleared, everyone was looking at Judy. She had stretched out her right arm, while an athletic looking brunette with professionally tangled curls positioned her. The massive rings on Judy's fingers trembled in anticipation.

"Head level with the floor. Eyes down," the brunette said, while the usual revelers watched respectfully.

"Don't say anything," Laura Collier whispered to me from her regular place at the bar. "You'll distract them."

Laura had puffy platinum hair that looked like it would break off in chunks if anyone touched it.

So I waved to Lillian for the house Merlot, hoping she'd put it on someone else's tab. Laura had a figure that befitted a barstool and a face that showed best in dim light.

"Say 'my name is Judy,'" the brunette said to Judy.

"My name is Judy."

The brunette pressed down on her outstretched arm. Nothing happened.

"Now say 'my name is Barry.'"

"My name is Barry," Judy said, giggling.

The brunette pressed her arm, and it dropped to her side. The people at the bar gasped.

"It's called muscle testing," Laura explained. "She's talking to Judy's subconscious."

For a second I thought Laura was going to muscle test a part of me. Then Judy saw us, and the spell was broken.

"Mel!" she cried, waving me to her. "This is my friend Tina."

Judy always introduced a new listing as "my friend." Tina had a face smoothed by plastic surgery and the widest smile cosmetic dentistry could manage.

"She does these wonderful seminars where you learn how to get in touch with your inner child and, well, Tina, you tell it," Judy said, retrieving her glass.

"It's called 'Deep Soul Plus' for depth psychology plus kinesthesia or muscle testing like chiropractors do?" Tina began with the rapid-fire delivery of the successful female realtor, then hesitated as if the house had termites or a leaky roof.

"Anyway, Mel, she's giving a seminar this weekend and she has a place open," Judy continued. "And you won't be the only man. Barry's going, too."

I knew what I had to do to get her agency's video business.

"You can put it on your credit card," Tina said reading my mind.

She had rented a junior high school gym on the other side of town for the session.

"And get home early," Judy said, glancing down the bar at Laura. "It starts at nine."

I had not been in a junior high gymnasium since the ninth grade, but nothing had changed: a rack of bleachers on one side, rolled up wrestling mats on the other, and the odor of gym shoes and sweat steeping in the steam heat. And there were the students, separated naturally into boys and girls teams, with Judy Revak and Laura Collier in their bright silk sweat suits dominating a tubby woman in jeans, and Barry Hunter, a car dealer and an insurance salesman sulking with the boys. If she had been wearing a whistle instead of an ankh, Tina would have blown it when I arrived. Instead she told us to sit down on the bleachers and handed each of us a packet of colored papers describing "Deep Soul Plus."

The first hour was a lecture that passed as slowly as an hour of calisthenics.

"What good does it do to go to therapy and learn about all your hang-ups, when you don't know how to get rid of them?" she said.

Perfume was oozing off the girls just as in eighth grade, and my eyes were so heavy that the huge score-keeping clock wobbled like a desert mirage.

"Your subconscious is a like a little child," she explained. "It only knows the present tense. We're going to learn how to talk to it and make it change its attitudes."

Then Tina told us to stand up, stretch, go to the bathroom, and we'd get started.

The paper towel holder in the boys' locker room was empty, so we had to use a towel Barry found under a bench.

"If I'd know what kind of a space she'd rented, I would have let her use my condo," Barry Hunter said.

"She'd look great on your water bed," the car dealer laughed.

"I thought of that," Hunter said as we loped back onto the floor like a losing team after half time. "What about you, Mel? Looking for a new face for one of your potty flicks?"

I didn't respond. According to the score-keeping clock, we had another six and a half hours to go.

"Small class?" Barry asked Tina as the girls emerged from their locker room, talking loudly and touching their hair.

"Just right," she said and divided us into twos, pairing Barry and the car dealer with Judy and the tubby woman, Laura with the insurance guy and me with her. Then she told the others to stand around us and had me stretch out my right arm at shoulder level. She smelled like herbs and Dial soap.

"First we test for strength. Say 'Yes,' Mel."

I heard Hunter and the car dealer snicker.

"Yes," I said, and she pushed gently down on my arm. It didn't move.

"Now say 'No,'" she said.

I said, "No," she pressed my arm, and it dropped to my side.

"Now the rest of you do it," she said.

She moved among them, helping to position their arms. Pair by pair, they tried "Yes" and "No." Arms held firm at "Yes" and dropped at "No."

Then she had us say our names, and our arms stayed up; then somebody else's name, and our arms all dropped. It was working.

"Here, Mel, try it on me," she said. "You have to learn how to do this, too."

That close to her, I could see the hair line cracks in her makeup and sensed something inside ready to snap if anything went wrong.

"It's all right to touch me," she said.

Her arm was taut when she said "Tina," but when she said her name was Mary, I just eased it to her side.

Then we asked our subconscious if it was ready to be balanced, and everybody's, even Barry Hunter's, said "Yes." We stretched out our arms again, and Tina told us to say: "I deserve to be happy and successful." Only Judy and Barry's arms stayed straight. Like a coach with a losing team, she made us sit down on the bleachers.

First she crossed our ankles and muscle tested to see whether the right or the left should be on top. Next she had us cross our wrists and muscle tested again to see which should be on top. Then we had to clasp our fingers with the wrists still crossed, like making an upside down "here is the church and here is the steeple."

"Now close your eyes," she said.

I felt like an accused murderer manacled to a courtroom chair. Hunter whispered something to Judy, and she giggled.

"Now say to yourself, 'I deserve to be happy and successful,'" Tina said. "Tell yourself all the reasons that you're not, but keep saying 'I deserve to be happy and successful' until you feel something."

"I deserve to be happy and successful," I said, and all the demons of a lifetime rushed out to say 'No!' and why not.

Cut from the high school basketball team, dropped out of film school, a failed marriage and *Lillian's Wine Bar* for a support group . . . But I deserve to be happy and successful. I deserve to be happy and successful! Then my neck and shoulders shuddered, my wrists and ankles tensed, and I glowed as if I'd won the lottery. I deserved to be happy and successful.

"Now uncross your ankles and wrists and put your finger tips together," Tina said, touching her fingers like a sorceress holding a crystal ball. "This locks it in."

Something had lifted: I was no longer in the gym where I had failed at jump shots twenty-five years earlier. I was in a safe, happy enclave from the late winter cold, warmed by the glow within. Instead of being surrounded by misfits and failures, I was setting off with pilgrims eager to experience new life. Barry was just one of the guys again, a kind of a jokester, and Judy the beauty-driven cheerleader.

The rest of the day was like breaking through a cloudbank at thirty thousand feet headed for California. One by one we identified each other's defeats and fears and weaknesses, drove them out, and cauterized the wounds. When the session was over, I didn't want to talk to anyone; I just wanted to go back to the apartment and think. For the first time in years, I had iced tea instead of beer with my TV dinner, then watched basketball on cable until I had calmed down enough to sleep. I couldn't wait for the next day.

On Sunday we switched partners, and I got Judy Revak. Barry's subconscious must have finally said "Yes" to something positive, because he was working happily with the tubby woman in jeans. Every phase of our lives was questioned, tested, corrected and sealed. By afternoon we were working on intractable problems, like binge eating for the women and booze for the guys. That's when Tina taught us the double sphere balance.

She lined us up in front of the bleachers like cheerleaders and had us raise and slap our thighs with the opposite hands, as if we were doing a junior high version of the Charleston. Judy popped a contact, and Tina had to hold up the exercise while she ran into the restroom to reinsert it. Then Tina told us to spread our arms wide, close our eyes and pretend we were holding the left side of our brains in one hand and the right in the other. The last thing I saw was Tina standing with her arms spread like Isis in her diaphanous gown, embracing the whole world.

"Now tell the two parts of your brain to embrace the new you."

I felt like an idiot telling one side of my brain to accept the idea that I didn't have to drink to have fun, until my arms started to move. Like a construction crane turning on a skyscraper, they swung together without any direction from me.

"Great, Mel!" Tina said. "Now put your fingers together and seal it in."

I had to sit down. The others' arms were coming together, and whatever had kept them from being happy and successful was finally exorcised. It was the most wonderful afternoon of my life.

At the end of the day, after Tina had taken an imprint of my credit card and promised not to send it through for a week, I was ready to shower up and begin my new life.

On the way to our cars, I arranged to pick up Judy for dinner somewhere; she was too tired to fix anything for herself. So I cleaned up, put on a fresh shirt and we had dinner at the café on the square. It felt like a date in college, when you mistake youth and excitement for compatibility and intelligence. We laughed about the weekend, about how Hunter wasn't as much of an asshole and Laura wasn't as pushy as everyone thought, and how great it felt finally to be free. I ordered a bottle of wine to celebrate, but neither us of had more than a sip. All I wanted was the cold hard clarity of water and the energy in my brain to surge on forever.

"I wonder if we should have a reunion sometime," I joked.

"I was going to suggest my place," Judy said.

It was the best sex in years. The next week was the most successful in my life: Judy called first thing Monday to say I had her business, and so did Laura. I was filming two houses a day all week. The next Monday, the director of the Contemporary Art Center called and said he wanted to do an installation featuring my virtual tours. He had heard about the bathroom foot from Barry Hunter, who said I was a genius. When I called Barry to thank him, he gave me his agency's virtual tour business, too. I even made my alimony and credit card payments on time and was looking forward to the rest of my life.

Several weeks later, when Judy had a late closing, I decided to drop by Lillian's to see if any of the old crowd was still there. In less than two months, the demographics had changed from over forty divorcees to kids fresh out of college, laughing loudly about what had happened at the office today or networking toward new jobs and new beds.

"Well, look who's back!" Lillian cried. "The house Merlot?"

"Just a Perrier," I said, and then I saw Tina.

She was sitting at the bar, staring at the wine in her glass.

"Maybe I will have the Merlot," I called to Lillian and edged past three bank trainees to Tina.

I caught her eyes in the mirror, the saddest, loneliest eyes I had ever seen.

"Has something happened?" I asked.

"I just sold my house, and I don't feel a thing."

I was stunned. Lillian set my wine on the bar, and Tina raised her glass to order another.

"I lived there twenty-three years, my daughter grew up there, I got divorced there, started all over again there, and now it's all gone and I don't feel a God damned thing!"

"Didn't you balance for it?" was all I could think to say.

"That's just the trouble, Mel. I balanced the hell out of it. I was ready for it. I could do it. And now it's like I'm under an anesthetic that just won't wear off."

She took the glass from Lillian and drank. For the first time since the junior high gym, I drank so I wouldn't have to talk.

"How can you stand this place?" she said. "Full of kids who don't even know what it's all about."

She was up and pushing her way to the door before I could catch Lillian's eye and call for our tabs. Tina had

had three glasses. I scribbled my signature on the credit card slip and hurried outside. She was standing by the mailbox at the curb.

"I am so damn sick of wine," she said.

"I still have a bottle of Vodka in the refrigerator."

"Mel, you're a lifesaver," she exclaimed, taking my arm in both hands as if we were about to balance.

I set the bottle and a glass on the tray table in the living room and waited for her to finish in the bathroom.

"You're not going to make me drink alone, are you?" she said when she saw the glass.

"We balanced so I wouldn't have to drink."

"You need to feel empathy with other people to be human," she said, taking my arm again. "Come on."

As professionally as in the junior high gym, she balanced me to enjoy a good drink with friends. I sat on the couch, crossed my ankles and wrists, but the long, deep shudder that meant that my subconscious had been reprogrammed did not come.

"Stand up," she said. "We'll have to do a hemisphere balance."

So I moved my legs up and down, slapping my thighs, until she told me to stand still and spread my arms. She smelled of burnt spices, the kind women let simmer in a pan on the stove until the water burns off.

"Just keep your eyes closed and think 'drink' on one side and 'friends' on the other."

I stood in the dark inhaling her bitter scent until my arms swung together so fast she jumped back. When my hands touched, my inner child rediscovered its taste for alcohol. She held my fingers together to lock it in.

She held my arm as I poured the icy cold Vodka into the glass. She had the first shot, I the second, and we watched the level sink like the sun over the ocean until the beach was dark and cold. When we went to bed, she was as numb as a sea creature left behind by the tide to glow and die on the hardening sand.

Midmorning bells awakened me, the heavy bells at the basilica calling the faithful to mass and the tinkling bells at the convent calling the sisters to prayers. But it wasn't Sunday in Florence, it was Tuesday in a gray Midwestern city, and the bells were my phone and cell calling antiphonally from both sides of the bed.

"Hello," I croaked into the cell, wondering if I had missed a video appointment.

"You bastard!" Judy Revak screamed. "You've been screwing Tina!"

I put the cell under Tina's pillow. It had a deep indentation as if something damp had curled up there for the night before slinking off just before dawn. Yes, Tina. She had something to do with this. Where was she?

"Answer me, you bastard!" Judy's tiny voice followed me to the bathroom.

I spent the day in the apartment, sipping tea and Ibuprofen, wondering why women had to confess to each other before their partner had awakened, and why the confessions never brought forgiveness.

Wednesday was better. I was able to eat an egg and load the equipment into the car for a job when my cell rang.

"Hey, man, what did you do to Judy?" Barry Hunter said. "I've never seen her so pissed."

"Yeah, well, you know, I think she's maybe out of balance."

"I don't know, Mel. We have a pretty good business relationship. I wouldn't want to piss her off."

So I took the equipment back to the apartment. I'd lost my two biggest clients in two days, and I didn't feel a thing. I deserve to be happy and successful. I'll just sit by the phone and wait for somebody else to call. After all, I had an installation going in at the Contemporary Art Center in two weeks. So I'll take a few days off to edit my tapes and rest up for all the new business.

The Director called late in the afternoon, after I'd had my first beer. They'd lost their funding. No exhibit. Too bad. You've got real talent. Maybe he could loosen up more money next year. Drop by some afternoon, and we'll have a drink.

I had the drink without him. Odd, to have your life disintegrate and be happy and unmoved, just like Tina. Most people drink so they won't feel anything; Tina and I drank to feel something, anything that was connected to the awful reality of our lives. I tried to call her, but her home number had been inactivated, and I didn't have her cell. Like a wanderer in the desert, she had rolled up her tent and disappeared. There was no one to talk to except my inner self, and my inner self was a child who only understood the present tense. Who could spend their life conversing with a three-year-old?

Like Tina, I knew the way out. I put the Vodka back into the refrigerator and found her brightly colored instruction sheets under my bills. If I could be balanced to be happy and successful, I could balance the other way. I sat down on the sofa, crossed my legs, linked my hands and told my self I deserved everything I got. Again the familiar rush, the shuddering relief, and the hot tears. Yes, I deserved everything that had happened.

I went through the other sheets, too, reversing a healthy life style, early morning awakening, bad food choices, intolerance of others, inability to sustain relationships, low regard for women, everything that had made me myself. When I was finished I was so exhausted I went to bed. At two-thirty in the morning I awoke, tormented by the rent and alimony and where I could find another job. The next morning I called my landlord. In another month he could put me in an efficiency on the fourth floor, and I would save enough to make the car payment.

The car dealer from the gym called on my cell and asked me to film his showroom and lot for his website. When we were finished, we went out for beers.

"Barry told me you're screwing Tina," he said admiringly.

"It really pissed Judy off," I replied.

"Don't worry about it, Mel. They're all alike."

And so are the rest of us. So I'm working more for car dealers now, making enough to get by and getting some good leads on a trade down to reduce my car payments, too. Sometimes, late in the evening, I drop by Lillian's for a few Merlots and to see who might show up. Judy Revak doesn't go there anymore. Laura can be a lot of fun after a closing, and one night I even scored with Lillian. She told me Tina bought the Deep Soul Plus franchise for St. Louis and had moved out of town.

Like me, however, Laura wakes up around three and can't get back to sleep.

"Maybe we should balance for sleep," I suggested after we had both been awake for an hour.

So she sat up on the edge of the bed and I balanced her. She didn't feel anything.

"Your turn," Mel," she said.

I stretched out my arm, and we balanced for "I go to sleep easily and wake up refreshed."

I crossed my ankles, folded my hands upside down and shut my eyes. Suddenly my neck muscles went into spasm, and I shook uncontrollably. From far away, I could hear Laura calling, "Mel? Mel!"

That's when I saw him, the red faced raging toddler, slick with tears and slobber, throwing his toys out of the playpen. He fixed me with a look of such loathing that I froze. Then he slammed against the slats, trying to reach me. If we touched, my heart would stop and I would die. Just as he was climbing over the side, Laura pulled my hands apart and broke the spell. I couldn't get back to sleep that night, not even after taking two Benadryl. Nothing is so hateful as a child you have betrayed.

So you can't go back to him a third time, thinking everything will be beautiful again. Laura is very good about that now. She just talks about how crazy all her clients are, and maybe she can find me some more work with other realtors. Her hair is not as brittle as I thought; it moves gently when I touch her. But we never talk about our inner children or what we really deserve.

THE DEER

Ideas are like cocaine. Touch a willing receptor, and the victim will never escape. We had gathered around the grill at the Harancourts' Labor Day party, drinking gin and tonics, and talking about the deer. At night they strolled across the lawn, snacking on bushes and plants. Then, like squads of marauding cavalry, they fanned out to terrify dogs, delight children and destroy every garden in our neighborhood.

"It's against the law to shoot them," Ty Renner the lawyer said.

"What about poison?" suggested Paul Kincaid, the orthopedic surgeon, who lived down the hill from Louise and me. He often came home late from the hospital and complained about deer in the road.

"You'd kill every dog in the neighborhood," retorted Angie Harancourt.

Mid forties, she sported the layered blond hair and glistening nails that distinguished habitués of the finest local salons. Working beside his father at the grill, her son Derek grimaced. Six months of family therapy with me had only intensified his hatred of his mother. When she arrived after a pedicure wearing cardboard tongs to separate her freshly varnished toes, I thought he would strangle on his disgust.

"I have a client in the suburbs who uses a crossbow," the lawyer said. "From up in the trees. It's perfectly legal."

"How horrible!" exclaimed Dawn Martin, a frazzled platinum blond with a flair for Jaguars and bathrobes during car pool. "What if the children saw?"

Derek smirked; he would love to watch someone shoot a deer with a crossbow.

"Then they've won," George Harancourt concluded, slapping another steak on the grill. Tall, hard eyed and brutally fit, the biggest developer in the city didn't like to lose. "The laws protect animals, not us."

I caught the edge in his voice, the driving, inconsiderate power that had shoved his wife aside and driven his son to drugs. Lacking his father's cunning and cruelty, Derek could only escape through cocaine.

"What about spears?" I said to turn it all into a joke.

"Right," laughed Eddie Martin, Harancourt's business partner. A foot shorter than George, Eddie mimicked him in everything: clothes, cars, a wife with the same build and hair, and a twin mansion overlooking the river. "The cops couldn't get us for that, could they, Ty?"

Their lawyer laughed and headed back to the veranda for another drink.

"The Humane Society would never allow it," Angie snapped.

Derek looked up from the grill, delighted to see his mother and his psychiatrist in conflict outside the office.

"It was just a joke, Angie," I said to calm her.

Then Louise turned the conversation to dahlias, and everyone seemed to relax. Sometimes my wife is better at group therapy than I; she had that worn, gray expression that distressed women find comforting. I wasn't even sure George had heard me, until we were lining up for the steaks.

"I know a guy who has a metal working shop," he said to me, lifting a T-bone onto my wife's plate. "I could ask him to make them."

"Make what?" asked Louise.

"The spears," he replied. "What about it, Carl?"

He looked straight at me.

"Are you in?"

Derek skewered a steak and held it over my plate.

Maybe it was the alcohol, maybe the night air, and maybe his damned arrogance to challenge me in front of my patient and my wife.

"Yes, George," I said. "I'm in."

"Great." He slapped my arm. "We'll talk later."

Derek dropped the steak onto my paper plate. It was so hot it burned my hand.

From the Harancourts' veranda, the terrace stretched like a dark green tarmac into the evening sky. Beyond lay the river valley, curling through the trees toward the downtown bridges. When the fireworks began, we watched the far away bursts like Valkyrie hovering over a battlefield. Fascinated, we forgot the hillside that sloped down to the parkway five hundred feet below, and the creatures that waited there for our little show to end.

As Louise and I walked home, we heard something behind us. Turning, we saw a huge stag, two does and four fawns trotting toward us.

"Look, Carl," she whispered, gripping my hand. "Aren't they beautiful?"

At the last minute they separated like dancers and passed us on both sides.

"How could anyone want to kill them?" she said.

"I was just joking, dear."

They disappeared ahead of us down the lane. When we got home, the dog was barking wildly.

After our dog Lonnie turned eight, he stopped going on walks with me. He refused to go outside unless Louise opened the door and said, "Look, Lonnie. There's a kitty!" There must have been something insincere in my voice; he wouldn't do that for me. One evening, after the dog had stayed in all day because of rain, we all went for a walk, Louise holding the leash. We were just turning around at the Harancourts' drive, when Derek came running down to us. Thin calves sticking out of his cutoffs, he looked like he should have spent the summer at band camp instead of rehabilitation.

"They're here!" he exclaimed. "Dad and Eddie are waiting. Come on!"

"What are you talking about, dear?" Louise asked.

"The spears, Mrs. Elliot. Come on!"

Derek ran up the lane toward the developers' mansions, as happy as when his father bought him a motorcycle for his sixteenth birthday. That was just before George went to Derek's room to tell him to turn down the stereo and caught him snorting cocaine.

"I thought you said it was a joke," Louise called back to me, as the dog pulled her after the teenager.

When I was a resident and she was a psychiatric nurse, her sympathetic listening attracted me. Twenty-five childless years later, however, the relationship had reversed. Now she spoke incessantly and I listened as long as I could, before moving away to do the dishes or find the TV program.

At the top of the lane, I saw Derek run across the lawn toward his father and Eddie Martin. They had set up a target on a bale of hay. While the two men talked, something in their hands flashed.

"This is ridiculous," whispered Louise as we approached.

"Try this one, Carl," Harancourt said, handing me a spear.

It had an ash shaft about four feet long and a beautifully shaped thin blade.

"It's for throwing," he explained. "The longer ones are for going one on one with them."

Both he and Martin held long thrusting spears with wide blades. Several throwing spears lay on the ground.

"Have you all gone out of your minds?" Louise exclaimed.

"I researched them," George continued, running his finger down the blood groove in the blade. "It's OK to touch it, Louise." He offered her the shaft. "It's surgical steel."

She recoiled as if he had offered her a serpent. He turned to me.

"Go ahead," Derek urged me. "Try it."

It almost throbbed in my hand.

"I'm taking Lonnie home," Louis snapped, jerking the dog away.

"Just like a football," Eddie Martin said.

"Did you hear me, Carl?" Louise called over her shoulder.

At the few parties or hospital functions we attended, that was her signal to disengage. I leaned back and threw the spear as hard as I could. For one lovely second it flew straight at the target, then dropped flat into the grass.

Louise laughed.

"You'd better stick to psychiatry," she said. "You'd never make it as a hunter."

Derek tried to catch my eye, but I looked away. I finally understood how a mother could taunt her son into addiction.

Like a coach with a player who missed an easy shot, George Harancourt put his hand on my shoulder.

"Like you're going for a long bomb," he said. "Watch."

He picked up a throwing spear, stepped back like a quarterback looking for a down field receiver and threw. The spear arched into the golden sunset and sliced into the white circle above the bull's eye.

"You're getting there," Eddie said.

He picked up another throwing spear and hurled it at the target, almost making up in force what his partner had in finesse. The spear struck the lower blue ring and hung quivering in the hay.

"Go get 'em, Derek," Harancourt called to his son.

The boy ran across the lawn to the target. When I looked around, Louise and the dog had disappeared. We spent the next hour practicing. Just before it got too dark, I hit the target on the outer ring, knocking the bale over.

"Way to go, killer!" Eddie Martin cried, and George slapped me on the shoulder.

As the new moon rose over the river valley, we sat on Harancourt's porch drinking beer. When I finally got home, Louise was in bed, and Lonnie was too tired to get up.

Everyone in the office commented on Derek's progress that fall. From a surly, sulky teenager he became a bright, focused young man, eager to share his enthusiasm for life. Only in the family sessions, when he and his father discussed the hunt while Angie raged between them, was the dynamic clear.

At home, Louise was elaborately calm. She addressed me in the same tone as I spoke to a recalcitrant patient in the office. The night I tried on my camouflage outfit and black hunting boots, she laughed at me again.

"What if your patients saw you now?" she sneered.

"Two of my patients will see me," I countered. "It's healing their relationship."

"What about our relationship?" she demanded in the same tone Angie used with Derek.

"It's just something to do in the evenings, Louise. Maybe if you were interested in the theater or music, we could do something together."

She looked at me as the deer would look the instant the blade struck home.

George, Eddie and Derek were waiting at the top of the lane with the spears. In the dull moonlight, I saw Harancourt and his son had black paint under their eyes.

"The wind is from the river," Harancourt said. "We'll wait here, where they can't smell us."

We spread out in the trees on both sides of the lane. Unless I had known the others were there, I could have been alone on the edge of the world. Hiding behind an oak, I held the spear against my chest. I had never known a night so quiet or excitement so intense. Sometimes I heard a car in the distance or a garage door opening. The only movements were blowing leaves. I was almost asleep when I heard Derek breath deeply. Coming toward us across the black terrace were two does and four fawns. They halted just out of range like soldiers on night patrol, each looking in a different direction. Satisfied they were alone, the larger doe stepped toward the lane.

The long bomb, Harancourt had said. Like a ballet dancer on a brightly lit stage, the doe could not see who was watching from the pit. Twenty yards, fifteen, I was drawing back to throw when two spears streaked through the moonlight. One plunged into her throat and the other struck her chest. Amazed, her front legs buckled, and she collapsed on her side. The others froze; how could the dark that nurtured them strike out? In that second, I threw my spear at the closest, saw it start and crumple, and felt the stomach-churning jolt of the kill. The other deer bolted for the hillside.

"You got one, Dr. Elliot, you got one!" Derek cried.

We ran to the deer. It was a fawn not four months old, panting and staring at us with wide black eyes, kicking at the shaft in its side with one hind foot. I had never seen anything so beautiful die.

"That was my kill," Harancourt said angrily to Eddie Martin. "She was in my zone."

"Don't get so bent out of shape," his partner replied sullenly.

"Dad!" Derek called. "Our deer won't die."

Harancourt came over, pulled out the spear and thrust it into the fawn's throat. Its flank stopped heaving, and everything relaxed.

"You should have waited until it was closer," he said.

"It's just a fawn," Eddie sneered.

"At least he made his own kill," Harancourt retorted.

He gripped the shaft so tightly his hand shook Men can share the same business, even the same woman, but not the same kill.

"Don't be so pissed off," Eddie said.

George threw the spear down and knelt beside the doe.

"I said I was sorry," Eddie sulked.

"Help me with this," Harancourt snapped. "We have to get it back to the garage."

The partners grabbed the doe's hind legs and started dragging her up the lane. Derek helped me lift the fawn onto my shoulders. Then he picked up the spears and followed us across the lawn. George and Eddie Martin stopped beside the garage.

"Let's finish the job," Harancourt said, drawing his hunting knife.

Eddie Martin drew his knife and knelt beside him.

While Derek watched, the developers gutted the doe without speaking. Then George handed his knife to his son and told him to do the fawn. The boy hesitated.

"You have to learn how to do it," his father said. "Watch."

Taking the knife again, Harancourt ripped the fawn open from the anus to the throat.

"Now you do it," he said.

Derek plunged both hands into the deer's entrails and lifted them onto the ground.

"Now let's have a contest and see who can skin their deer fastest," Harancourt said.

Neither Derek nor Eddie Martin had ever skinned a deer.

"Cut around the neck and the shoulder, just like you're unzipping its coat," Harancourt said.

Derek wasn't strong enough to pull the hide off by himself. His father knelt beside him to hold it down while I yanked the skin off. I had never seen them so close.

"Isn't anybody going to help me?" Eddie complained.

Without speaking, George held the doe until his partner had yanked off its skin. While Eddie Martin and Derek were stuffing the guts into garbage bags, George and I hung the carcasses in the air-conditioned workroom to drain and cure. Then we sat on Harancourt's front steps and drank beer.

"You did real good for a beginner, Doc," George said as I stood up.

Leaving the spear and the carcass with Derek, I shuffled down the lane like a lineman singled out by the quarterback after a close game.

I had never been so tired when I got home. When I went upstairs and turned on the lamp on my dresser, Louise was still awake.

"What have you done?" she gasped.

My hands and arms were black with blood.

"Don't ever touch me again," she said.

That fall I learned how to grill. While Louise picked at a salad or talked on her cell phone with her support group, I grilled venison on the deck and drank beer. In the office I finally understood why so many of my male patients knew more about barbecue sauce than about their families. Asking for a recipe was a better way to build a therapeutic alliance than delving into their deepest secrets, where every shared shame only separated us farther. Even the dog came outside with me again after I started tossing him scraps. When it was too dark to read, I changed into my fatigues and went hunting.

My practice started to change, too. When Derek and his parents came in for therapy, the boy and his father moved their chairs close to me. Angie, isolated, refused to participate.

"If you're just going to talk about hunting again, I'm leaving," she said.

Derek and his father were silent. There was nothing they wanted more than for her to leave.

"It's better to talk about something Derek is passionate about," I said.

Angie stalked out. Harancourt looked like I'd just saved his son's life, and I felt the same wild relief as when I passed my boards and would never have to take another test again. Derek smiled. Like a judo fighter matched against an implacable opponent, he had finally found how to break her hold.

We laughed and talked for the rest of the hour. As I walked them to the door, George had his arm around his son's shoulder. On our next hunt I took George aside and told him they didn't need to come back again. Derek made his first kill that night. With his father and me watching proudly, he slit it open, splashing himself with the rich warm blood.

I will never forget the night I got my first stag. Harancourt had stationed us in the trees above the lane like a picket line in the dark ages. Derek stood just a little to the rear with a thrusting spear in case one broke through. It was Indian summer, and I was sweating through my fatigues. Then a cloud slid away from the moon, and the deer emerged from the night like an unfamiliar shadow on an x-ray. Disbelieving, we stared into each other's eyes. Slowly, slowly, I was drawing back to throw, when a car turned onto the road below us. The stag realized he was not alone and leapt to the side as I threw. The spear caught him in the left shoulder. Like a running back hit by a lineman, he stumbled, then darted forward. Derek lunged out of the dark, but the deer zigzagged around him and sprang down the hill.

"Shit!" Derek cried. "I missed him!"

A hard thump! Breaking glass and the car swerved and crashed, bathing us in its headlights.

"Come on!" I cried, and we ran through the trees toward the lights.

Paul Kincaid's Lexus had leapt into the hillside and smashed its beautiful grill into a tree. Something covered the windshield.

"It's the deer," Derek said.

The buck was upside down across the hood, its head turned backwards into the broken windshield. I ran to the door.

"Paul!" I cried, yanking it open.

Mouth open, he was staring into the dead stag's eyes. "Paul?"

I touched his shoulder, but he didn't move. Then I saw the antlers had pierced his chest.

"Son of a bitch," Eddie Martin whispered.

We heard another car coming up the road. Harancourt reached inside and turned off the lights. Stepping back, he pulled the spear out of the deer's shoulder.

"Go home through the woods," he said.

We all understood what he meant. Hunting accidents are difficult to explain when the intended prey kills a bystander. Ty Renner's legal system would never understand that the thrill of the hunt is more important than any one life.

The dog must have known I was coming through the yard and didn't bark. Maybe the blood and the fear silenced them, too. Red and white lights were flashing through the trees, and the police radio grated loudly in the fall air.

"Have you killed someone?" Louise demanded as I climbed into bed.

I didn't answer.

"I'm leaving you, Carl," she continued. "I have a lawyer."

"Do you want the house?" I asked for something to say.

"No," she replied. "But I'm taking the dog."

That was the longest night in my life, lying there listening to her sob. I got up early to let Lonnie out, but he cringed at the door.

"Get the kitty!" I yelled savagely, and he bounded into the yard.

"You don't have to yell at him," Louise said, clutching her housecoat to her breasts. "Here, Lonnie," she called from the door. "Mommy's here. It's okay."

Several minutes later, the dog loped onto the porch carrying the Renners' cat in his jaws.

"Keep him," she screamed. "I never want to see anything that reminds me of you again!"

That was the last time Louise spoke to me. She moved into a friend's apartment that afternoon. When I saw her at Paul Kincaid's funeral, she turned away before I could make eye contact. I found an empty place beside Dawn Martin. Neither of the developers was at the church.

"You were with George and Eddie that night, weren't you?" she whispered.

Her eyes were red and her makeup smeared from crying. I nodded.

"It's all right," she said, taking my hand. "I shouldn't have been there, either. It's a judgment on all of us."

She gripped my hand throughout the service. When Lori Kincaid walked out after the casket with her children, Dawn leaned against my shoulder and sobbed. I had read in the newspaper that she had found him, but I didn't realize until then that he had not been in surgery that night.

"I'd be happy to see you, if you think it would help," I said.

"Thanks, Carl." She squeezed my arm. "I think it would."

When word got out that Louise and I had separated, I lost most of my female patients. I hadn't realized so many of them were her friends. In their place came men from drop in centers, veterans, and court referrals for domestic violence. The waiting room smelled of sweat and alcohol. First my social worker, then another therapist left, so I had to do most of the groups myself.

We talked in the conference room until the smoke burned our eyes, and our memories were raw. Middle-aged men who had crept through jungles at night to strangle their enemies with piano wire traded stories with younger men who had waited outside motels for hours to catch their wives with their lovers. Toward the end, they always turned to me, saying: "And what about you, Doc?"

Then I told about the spears arching towards the deer. For them it unlocked memories of firing a grenade launcher over the rice fields toward a running man, or mortar shells dropping from the sky. It was the moment of the kill, when every nerve was stretched thin and time stood still that bound us together. After that, who could drive a truck or pay alimony or stop drinking, when the drink might blot it out or, even better, bring it all rushing back?

After a late night session, my office manager found beer cans in the conference room and quit. My last female therapist and one of the clerks left then, too.

"Go to hell," I cried after them in my mind.

Shifting my practice from HMOs and private pays to Medicaid and Medicare meant they had to go, anyway. Better for everyone if they thought it was over an issue, not just money. Only when the beer went flat and my throat was sore from the smoke did I sense the emptiness at the center of it all. Why did we always have to talk? Why isn't life enough? What was it that kept calling us back to death, luring us to challenge it again? Why couldn't we face it and kill it, once and for all? Even when I made love to Dawn Martin, it was more for the thrill of taking the wife of a man who hunted with a spear than from any passion for her.

On a beautiful fall evening, I was on the deck grilling venison, when the dog pressed against me.

"You'll have to wait," I said.

He whined and pawed my leg.

"What?" I said and turned.

A seven point stag stood on the lawn like a thoroughbred in the winners' circle. I had never seen anything so beautiful and so arrogant. Then I recognized him: the stage who pranced past Louise and me after the Labor Day picnic. The bastard knows we've given up, I thought. It saw me, the man, helpless, with my dog cringing against my legs.

"Damn you!" I cried, hurling the cooking fork at him.

It struck the ground at his feet. He didn't move.

Furious, I ran into the house for my spear. Despite slamming doors and the dog, it just stood there, watching.

Couldn't he see what I was doing? When I stepped onto the deck again, he was nibbling the last of the lilies. I mattered so little he didn't bother to look up.

"You bastard!" I cried, cursing the dull indifference that mocks and breaks the best men.

Like a German Shepherd taunted by a lap dog, he raised his head slowly. Not even the smell of venison smoldering on my grill bothered him. Amused, he cocked his head as I drew back and hurled the spear. It flew like a finely thrown fastball and cut through the base of his neck into his chest. He blinked once and dropped onto his side. The evening was so still I could hear when his breath stopped.

It was the finest night of my life, with the venison and the beer and the body of my enemy at my feet. When it was dark, I called Derek to ask if he'd help me dress a deer. His father answered.

"I thought we weren't going to do that anymore," he said.

"I had to," I replied and told him how the buck had mocked me.

When Derek arrived, I turned on the back yard lights.

"Where is it?" he asked.

The yard was empty. The boy looked at me as if I was the patient. I went into the kitchen for a flashlight, and we went down the hill.

"It was there," I said, lighting a shiny patch on the grass.

He knelt and touched the ground.

"You got one, all right." His fingers were wet and sticky. "Let's follow it."

"Your father wouldn't want you to."

I had never seen him so disappointed.

"Maybe we should just let it die in the woods, Derek."

And that's what I thought it did. The next day I worked late and bought a casserole and a bottle of wine on the way home. The message light on the telephone was on. Maybe it would be another good night; the only one who left me messages was Dawn.

"Carl," Dawn's voice said. "It was here this afternoon. You have to do something about it. Call me."

I called three times before she answered.

"It was the one that killed Paul," she insisted.

"That's impossible," I said. "It's been dead for weeks."

"It's not dead, Carl. It still has your spear sticking out of it."

"Maybe one of the others," I said.

"Just do something. I can't stand it. You'll have to kill it."

She hung up.

How long could a deer live with a wound like that? Maybe I should call George Harancourt. He'd know what to do. But what would Harancourt think of a man who couldn't finish his own kill? I couldn't let it shame me. Let it die by itself.

The next evening when I got home, the message light was off. Good, I thought. It's dead. I was opening a beer when the doorbell rang. A man in a windbreaker and a uniformed policeman were on the porch. My God, I thought. Derek's done something terrible. Fighting back fear, I opened the door. They seemed uncomfortable with Louise's Chinese wallpaper in the vestibule, but they didn't want to sit down. I had heard from my patients that they acted this way when someone had died.

"I didn't want to call the office, Doctor," the detective said. "I don't like to worry people."

"Is it about Derek?"

The Detective glanced at the uniformed officer.

"Mrs. Kincaid saw a deer in her yard when her kids were getting off the school bus," he said. "There was a spear sticking out of its chest."

I was still holding the beer, and there was nowhere to put it down.

"Funny thing," the uniformed officer said. "When they checked out the deer that killed Dr. Kincaid, there was a wound in its shoulder, like it had been stabbed or something."

"There's a rumor in the neighborhood that some guys have been hunting deer with spears," the detective continued. "You hear anything about that?

"I hadn't heard that," I said, sweating through my shirt.

The detective looked at the uniformed officer.

"That's funny. Somebody told us you were talking about it at the Harancourts' Labor Day picnic."

"Oh, that," I said. "That was just a joke."

"That's what I would have thought, too, Doctor", the detective concluded, looking at the uniformed officer again.

"You have anything else?" I said.

The policeman shook his head.

"Okay, Doc. Have a nice night."

I stood in the vestibule staring at the Chinese wallpaper. Near the mountains in the distance, heads cocked toward the painter, were several deer.

George Harancourt did not have the officers' hesitancy about disturbing me at work.

"Angie just called," he said. "Your deer was at the house."

"It's still there?" was all I could think to say.

"She saw it go down over the hill."

My patients were arguing in the conference room.

"George, I have to get back to work," I said.

"We're going after it. Tonight. Together. Meet me at the house at nine."

In the conference room, a Vietnam veteran was shaking a drug dealer against the wall.

"Don't call me brother!" he screamed.

We started down the hillside single file like Indians: first the developers, then Derek, and then me. The moon disappeared over the ridge, and we crept forward in nearly perfect darkness. Suddenly Derek slipped, and a torrent of stones rushed over the drop off. Everyone stopped. My fingers were numb with cold. As we started forward again, I saw the yellow streetlights along the parkway five hundred feet below. Fear gripped my chest like ice.

Two hours later we found their trail. It's something you sense when the brush starts to separate, and you feel yourself entering a blacker V in the night. We were moving easily when the path widened, and we found them huddled beneath an overhang. Like freshly conjured spirits, the fawns stared at us with startled eyes too new to the world for fear. The does huddled around the huge stag as if to shield him, while a young buck stepped between the herd and us. As Harancourt waved us into a semicircle, the old stag brushed the does aside.

Derek gasped. The spear was still hanging from his chest.

You can also sense when another man is going for your kill.

"He's mine!" Harancourt hissed to Eddie Martin.

As the stag started toward us, their eyes met. Both men were leaning back into their throws, but I was quicker. My spear struck the stag in the chest. George's spear sliced across his neck, and Eddie's caught the young buck in the shoulder joint. He spun into the air like Baryshnikov and bolted down the trail as the old stag sunk to his knees. The fawns and does scattered past us like early morning dreams. I started towards the stag.

"You bastard!" Harancourt yelled at me. "I told you he was mine!"

"Fuck you!" Eddie Martin cried, pushing Harancourt's chest with both hands. "The world doesn't belong to you!"

George hit him in the mouth.

"You fucking bastard!" Eddie screamed, drawing his hunting knife.

Mad with fear and pain, the wounded buck crashed into a tree and turned back towards us.

Harancourt backed toward the old stag, reaching for his hunting knife, as the wounded buck came bounding toward him. Seeing his chance, Eddie Martin lunged at his partner. The buck saw the movement and swerved, catching Eddie on his antlers and raising him upside down. For a second they looked into each other's eyes. Then Eddie slashed at his throat with his knife, and the deer collapsed on top of him.

"Help me!" Eddie cried. "For God's sake, help me!"

Drooling blood, the buck thrashed madly, driving them toward the drop off. Eddie arched backward with all his strength as he struggled to break free. At the last second, he twisted out of the antlers, but the slope was too steep and the ground too hard to hold.

"Shit," said Eddie Martin, watching his fingers slip.

His knife slid over the edge and dropped into the darkness.

"For a deer," he cursed us. "All for a fucking deer!"

He flailed at the branches, then dropped screaming toward the parkway. In the sudden silence, the buck looked at us like a startled child who made baby cry with a kiss. Derek started toward him with his spear.

"Don't kill him," Harancourt said. "We have to make them think Eddie did this all himself."

Every few seconds, the young buck twitched and kicked at the spear in its shoulder.

"Come on. We'll just slide him over after him. Watch those hooves, Derek."

Derek was shoving the buck toward the edge with the shaft of his spear, when I saw the big stag move.

"George," I tried to warn him.

"Fuck you," he said.

Head down, the stag came at him on three legs.

"Derek!" he cried, as the antlers knocked him down. "Derek!"

He slid toward the drop off like a swimmer caught in an undertow, pumping his beautiful catalogue boots for a foothold. As his feet slipped away, he drew his hunting knife and stabbed it into the hillside. His free hand reached out like a trapeze artist the instant before the catch is missed.

"Help me, son!" he cried.

Derek knelt and held out the shaft to him. The stag's blood oozed down over Harancourt's fingers.

"Dr. Elliott," Derek pleaded. "I can't hold it."

I grabbed a tree with one hand and his arm with the other. Leaning on the knife, Harancourt grabbed the shaft with his other hand and started to pull himself up. As he rose, he placed one foot on the knife.

"Hurry, Dad," Derek sobbed.

Then Harancourt had both hands on the shaft and was pushing himself up with his free foot. The weight was off the spear; Derek leaned back, gasping for breath. Harancourt was almost to his son when the darkness shifted, and the old stag lurched to his knees.

"Dad!" Derek screamed.

With one last shuddering breath, the stag lunged between the developer and his son, breaking the boy's grip on the spear.

"Dad!"

Harancourt stood straight up on one leg on the knife. Slowly, slowly, he leaned backwards into the darkness. One hand held the spear, the other still reached out for his son. Eyes searching the darkness for Derek's face, he fell.

"Damn you!" Derek screamed, drawing his knife.

He dove on the stag like a wrestler, rolling it onto its back.

"Derek!" I cried. "Derek!"

Sirens rose from the parkway, but the boy drove the knife in again and again. He would not stop, not even when flashlights swept through the trees, and the officers called down to us. If they had not pulled him off and taken the knife, he would have died there, too, frozen in the animal's blood.

I still see Derek at an institution for long term care where he will probably spend the rest of his life. It has a campus atmosphere, with spacious dormitories and classroom buildings, and a gatehouse on the drive. From his room you can barely see the fence topped with concertina wire that separates him from the world. Derek likes to look at the wire, because it makes him feel safe. Angie found a service that sends him presents at Christmas and birthdays, and checks every six months to see if he has outgrown his clothes.

If he were able to sleep, his prognosis would be better. Night after night he keeps himself awake, afraid that if he dreams of our last hunt, he will drop into death like his father. If I could teach him to rejoice in the moment he lost everything that bound him to the earth, he would be free. He would be healed. But if I could do that, I would be God.

So I lead group sessions, and grill steaks outside in summer, and wonder if we have all died and gone to hell. At the end of our sessions, my patients always ask me to tell them the story about the boy and his father and the deer, like children demanding the same bedtime story night after night. Somehow this wards off the despair where the nightmares form. I cannot forgive their sins; I can only share my own. So I tell them the story to help them sleep, but I know they will never escape.

There is no one left to hold a neighborhood party. The people who bought the developers' houses are very private. Dawn is engaged to a dot.com entrepreneur and only calls when he is out of town. I have thought about looking for another woman, but then I have a drink and realize it is better for me to be alone. Some nights I walk up the lane to look down at the parkway and wish there were some way I could make it all come back. Then I remember Derek and my veterans and go to bed. I am eager for the dreams to come.

A FRIEND OF
BILL GILLEN

For a real estate agent, hell is a silent phone. You sit at your desk pretending to have something to do, while the big producers usher their clients in and out of their private offices and rush off to six figure closings. You're lucky if they ask you to put up a yard sign at one of their new listings or hand out circulars at an open house. And all the time you're thinking, what am I going to do if I can't make it on commission? How long until the credit cards are maxed out, the eviction notice is slipped under the door, and Martha's lawyer is after me again for criminal contempt?

I asked Darrell Williams, the agency's biggest producer, the secret of his success. Elegant in blue blazer, white silk shirt, gray slacks and alligator loafers, he was chatting with the secretary by her desk. She had slipped off her shoes and was touching the side of his foot with her toe. Darrell wasn't wearing socks. With two new million dollar plus listings in the paper that morning, he was feeling expansive.

"Come into my office," he said, putting his hand on my shoulder and rolling his eyes at the secretary. "I'll show you my secret weapon."

He had an enormous desk and mahogany paneling covered with plaques for the years he had been a member of the ten million-dollar roundtable. Smiling, he reached into his bottom desk drawer and pulled out a little plastic statue of a bearded man in a robe and sandals.

"Here," he said. "Know what this is?"

I shook my head.

"It's a statue of Saint Joseph. Bury it upside down in the front yard when you put up the for sale sign. It guarantees a quick sale."

"What if you don't have any listings?" I asked.

"Then you better find another place to bury it," he said.

He was laughing so hard the other part timers in the telephone room and the secretary looked up as I left his office.

That afternoon I was the only left in the office. All the others were out at showings and closings; even the secretary had gone home early. So I read the listings again and again, so afraid I'd miss a call that I only left the room to go to the bathroom. Just as I opened the door to the telephone room, I heard the last ring. I ran to my desk, but the message light was dark. Of course it wasn't for me.

If I hadn't been desperate, I would have sat down and just kept hoping, and none of this would have happened. Instead I looked at the secretary's phone. Her message light was dark, too.

The call had to have gone somewhere. I went up and down the aisles in the telephone room. All the phones were dark. So I looked in the manager's office, then the big producers'. Nothing. Last was Darrell Williams'. His phone was on the credenza behind his desk, and his message light was on.

I picked up the phone, pressed "messages", and a voice asked me to enter my password and the pound sign. Password? All I had was the office password, only good for the telephone room.

"Sorry. Try again," the voice said.

Beside the phone, mocking me, was a picture of Williams and his huge BMW with his personalized license plate, "Beamer1."

"That's it!" I thought, entered "Beamer1," and hit pound.

"You have one message," the voice said.

"This is Kevin Angel. I'm a friend of Bill Gillen," a soft male voice said. "My address is 2750 Brite Drive. Bill said you'd handle everything. There's a key in the mailbox. Leave the listing agreement, and you can pick it up tomorrow. Try to get a hundred fifty, but I have to get out of here. Leave a voice mail at 274-5650 when I have to sign something else."

I was clear headed enough to write everything down and erase the message. When the manager returned from depositing a commission check, I told him I had to talk to a guy about a new listing. He looked as if he didn't believe me.

2750 Brite Drive was a split-level, brick down, white siding up, in a sixties subdivision a few miles from an aging shopping center. The only thing that distinguished it from its neighbors was the lack of plastic toys in the yard. Sure enough, the key was in the mailbox. I went in to measure the rooms.

A guy like me, I thought. Hardly any furniture except a TV and couch in the living room, a table and three chairs in the dinette, and a bed and another TV in one of the bedrooms. The bathroom hadn't been cleaned in months. So I get someone to cut the grass, a cleaning service for the bathrooms, and it's perfect for the typical American family of four. The only unusual feature was a dead bolt lock on the basement door on the kitchen side.

Maybe he keeps pit bulls, I thought, and knocked, half expecting something to rush up the stairs and slam into the door. Silence. I opened the door and went downstairs. There was a fetid smell, as if someone had left cat food out too long. When I turned on the light, however, I forgot all about it. The most elaborate model railroad I had ever seen filled the recreation room. So that's why the rest of the place is so empty. I left a note about the grass and the cleaning service attached to the listing agreement and went home for my first decent night's sleep in weeks.

A real estate agent's dream is a new listing, sure to sell plus attract other listings in the neighborhood. For the first time, the other agents looked at me like I might be able to do something besides answer the phone and go for sandwiches at lunch. Then the calls started from people and other agents who had seen the ad and wanted to see the house. I finally had something to do.

The Brimleys were the perfect Brite Drive couple. She was a few months pregnant, he was an electrical engineer at a near by plant, and they had met at a model railroad convention.

"What's the smell?" was Mary Jo's only critical question.

"He used to have a cat," I said.

"Hey, honey," Todd Brimley called from behind the furnace. "There's a crawl space."

I hadn't noticed that. Mary Jo looked at me expectantly.

"Keeps the heat off in summer," I told her.

By the time we caught up with Todd, he was squatting by the water heater, studying its specifications.

"What do you think, honey?" he said, standing up.

"Let's go upstairs and talk," she replied.

I told them I expected a contract from another couple that evening, so they'd better move fast. As soon as they were gone I stepped behind the furnace and, sure enough, there was a crawl space. The smell was stronger, as if someone had dropped a bag of fast food in and forgotten about it. I went to the train room for a flashlight.

Upstairs the Brimleys were talking excitedly like a young couple making love. When you've made the sale, shut up, all the pros say. So I stood on tiptoes and shined the light into the crawl space. My stomach froze. Sticking out of the dirt at the back was a human foot.

"Hey, Art!" Todd called down from the kitchen. "We're ready!"

I couldn't move. My first listing, my first sale, and my career was ruined. For the rest of my life I'd be the guy who showed houses with bodies in the basement. And if I didn't sell that house, I was looking at thirty days in jail for contempt of my divorce decree.

"Art? What are you doing? Playing with the trains?" Todd called again.

"I'm coming," I said, returning the flashlight to the train room and going upstairs.

Mary Jo hugged me, and they signed a contract for the asking price. I left Kevin Angel a note to sign the contract and clean the place up, especially the basement before the closing.

I don't know how I got through the next two weeks. When Mary Jo called to ask if she could show the house to her mother, I nearly panicked.

"I'll ask the owner," I said.

It's all over now, I thought. No one is more critical that the buyer's mother. She'll smell the body, look in the crawl space and call the police. I called Kevin Angel's number and left a message that the buyer and her mother wanted to see the house again, and he'd better get it cleaned up fast.

"And for God's sake, do something about that smell!" I pleaded.

It was the longest afternoon of my life. Every time the phone rang, I thought it was Kevin. There was a call from a woman on Brite Drive thinking about divorcing her husband and wanting to know how much they could get for the house.

"A hundred seventy-five for sure," I said. "My last listing there went in two days."

Ten minutes later, the soon to be ex-husband called. He couldn't believe a hundred seventy-five thousand. While I was telling him I had sold the house three doors down for the asking price, the phone chirped and the message light went on. I couldn't get the guy off the line. In my experience, a rising real estate market has broken up more marriages than adultery. Finally, after I promised to come out that night with a listing agreement, he hung up. Chest tightening, I hit my voice mail button.

"Thanks for all you're doing for me," Kevin Angel's voice said. "Bill was right about you. You can take Mary Jo and Mother to the house tomorrow afternoon. They'll love the basement."

They did love the basement. Everywhere, even behind the furnace, was the smell of lemon cleanser. The bathrooms were clean, and the soap scum had vanished from the chrome strips in the tile. While Mary Jo and Mother were admiring the electric trains, I took the flashlight and peered into the crawl space. All I could see was freshly smoothed dirt.

Kevin Angel arrived late at the closing, complaining of his short lunch hour at the library. Pale, pudgy, in khaki wash and wears with a partially untucked blue shirt and polyester tie, he watched happily as the woman from the bank passed paper after paper to the Brimleys. When it was time for him to sign the deed, he took a deep breath. Then the woman from the bank handed us our checks, we shook hands with the Brimleys, and they left the conference room holding hands. I had never had so much money before in my life.

"Bill sure was right about you," my client said, after the woman from the bank had bundled up her papers and departed. "Would you like to get together for a drink? I get off at five."

"Love to, but I have a showing down the street from your old place," I excused myself.

"Too bad. I wanted to get to know you better."

We left the bank in opposite directions. In our brief time together, we did not shake hands. On the way to the parking garage, I dropped off a certified check for back alimony to Martha's lawyer. For the first time since I met her, I was free. I never saw Kevin Angel again.

I did, however, hear from other friends of Bill Gillen. Sometimes they wanted to talk about a house before I showed it, but usually they preferred the anonymity of a key in the mailbox. Kevin was the only one I ever had to tell to clean his place up. All the other houses smelled of lemon cleanser when I first arrived, although I sometimes caught a whiff of cat food in unvented spaces.

When I was elected to the ten million-dollar round table, I tried to call Bill Gillen. I wanted him to attend the awards dinner as my guest. He must have had an unlisted number, and I didn't want to ask any of his referrals. Sometimes the best way to service a big client is to just do the job and let the golf games go. I change the password on my office voicemail twice a week to keep others from disturbing my relationships.

Our agency moved into a larger space so I could have an office bigger than Darrell Williams', and my own secretary. I have a Mercedes Benz Maibach bigger than his Beamer, too. Best of all, Martha and her lawyer are eating their hearts out, because my five hundred-dollar an hour lawyer got the judge to cut her alimony in half. She just wasn't trying hard enough to find a job, the court ruled.

Now I read the second section of the newspaper, where they report the daily killings in the inner city and disappearances in the suburbs, as eagerly as I read the new listings. Can there really be a group that buries their victims in their basements and gardens, and uses the same real estate agent when the plot is full? According to the paper, there aren't many missing bodies. The only delay is when they have to drag the river. Who, then, do Kevin Angel and his colleagues bury in their crawl spaces? And if nobody misses them, does it really matter that they are dead? Is death as unreal as the sound of a tree falling in the forest, when there is no one to hear it?

These are the questions I ask myself, when I have an empty moment between phone calls and closings, or when I wake up in the middle of the night, or the sleeping pills don't work. Once at the office Christmas party, I almost asked Darrell Williams. His production was off and he looked so unhappy I just left him with the scotch and tortilla chips. Besides, the secretary was after me for some more champagne.

So Bill Gillen remains a mystery, like the statues of Saint Joseph. I've never had anyone say they don't work. Whatever he may be to others, Bill has always been magic for me.

LILLIAN

Her name, I think, is Lillian. At least that's what I call to her in dreams. She is not so much a person as a presence, a warmth that awakens me when I try to touch her. How strange to feel such longing for someone who may never have existed. She is like a name that you recognize but cannot place, a thought detached from words.

The rest of my life is very organized. A young man in a puffy blue gown and large white gym shoes awakens me at seven. It is more like a game we play. I am always awake wondering what has happened to Lillian and just pretend to be asleep when he opens my door. There are always such loud noises in the hall, carts and trays and funny smells, and large, happy people in puffy blue gowns calling greetings to one another.

If I have had a good night, he helps me out of my plastic wrappings and to the toilet and then the shower, where he sprays me with warm water. If I have had a bad night, well, we do the same things, but he sprays me first and talks to himself about why he gets all the nasty ones. When I tell him about my dreams, he says, "At your age? No way!"

At least that is what I think he says. It has been a long time since we have really communicated. Our last discussion was about shoes. He likes gym shoes; I prefer slippers. Since they are my feet, I can turn them away when he tries to put gym shoes on them. So he told on me to an overweight woman with a clipboard in her hand. I haven't worn gym shoes since I was a child, I thought so hard I was sure she could hear.

"He won't wear shoes," my caregiver complained. "Acts like he's tryin' to kick my ass."

"Let him wear his slippers," the large woman said. "He ain't runnin' no marathon here, honey."

That's one of the few I have won in a long time. If Lillian were here, we would laugh about it together. Maybe she is down the hall, where they are lining up the residents in wheelchairs for their turns at breakfast. It is incongruous to see so many old people in wheelchairs wearing gym shoes. They are hard to put on, and none of the residents can bend over to tie the laces.

Meals are difficult. Everyone seems to concentrate on something that is happening somewhere else. People stare across the room, or at their food, or chew without putting anything in their mouths. Breakfast is the worst meal to watch other people eat. I think about Lillian until our time is nearly over and the food is cold. It is difficult to eat a cold breakfast in a hurry, but if you don't, they put your name on a list and give you an injection instead. It hurts when they put in the needle, but there are benefits to not eating. The less I eat, the fewer bad mornings I have.

Somewhere there was a kitchen that smelled of bacon and coffee, and a young woman with brown hair wearing an apron over her fresh spring dress. She smiles at me while she stirs the pancake batter with the new electric mixer, and the children argue happily about who will be served first. Black headlines scream about war in Korea, but when she smiles, the world is soft and light.

If you are good and eat your breakfast, they take you to the sunroom, where there is a television set. The people in blue gowns like to watch shows where overweight people sit around a stage and yell at each other. If the staff here and television shows are any indication, fat people have taken over the country.

Sometimes the people on television start hitting each other, but they are so fat that no one is ever hurt. People watching from an amphitheater yell, "Jerry, Jerry!" That must mean, "Hit them harder," because the people on stage keep right on pounding. Then come the commercials, where everybody is normal size again. So maybe the fat people haven't taken over the country after all. Maybe it's just here. Lillian would know, if I only knew where to find her.

Some of us get to go to the bathroom before lunch and some after. I wish I could remember which group I am in. If you forget, your caregiver has to take you back to your room and stand you in the shower again while he talks to himself and rummages through your dresser for clean clothes.

Today lunch is beef barley soup and enchiladas. I used to go to a place where they served Mexican food and cloudy green drinks that tasted like salt and lime. Mr. Jasper, who sits across from me at lunch, may have been thinking the same thing. In the evening we would sit outside on the patio and talk about ships and worry about ever finding the right girl. I tried to imagine Mr. Jasper in a white uniform with gold epaulettes. Neither of us touched our beef barley soup.

I knew Mr. Jasper or someone like him, or maybe another person altogether during "the War." But which war was it? We were junior officers on the same ship, but whether the ship was gray metal with a white number on her bow, or she was wood and had a painted goddess on her prow, I no longer remember. Perhaps we fired broadsides from huge guns at tiny green atolls, while airplanes with red circles on their wings banked towards us through black bursts of flack. Another time we built towers on our troop ships, so when the Carthaginian galleys swept alongside, we could shower them with arrows. Who could forget the brilliant blue sea and white sand that circled the harbor, but where was the harbor? San Diego? Piraeus? Nothing matters except the smell of the fresh sea air, which I shall never taste again.

"They sure like them enchiladas," said a large young woman, who helps us to eat when we become distracted. "Just like we're in Tijuana."

Mr. Jasper and I smiled, and I picked up my enchilada before she could cut it for me. No, he is not Ulysses; no Penelope awaits him here. He has drunk from Circe's cup and will never again awaken. But I have sipped the liquor of the gods and danced with a nymph on the edge of the sea. Whether it was at Ensenada or Ostia makes no difference now.

We drank the salty green liquid and ate enchiladas with our fingers, then rinsed our hands in the surf and ran along the beach until the sun set. She was so beautiful, so tan, so close and so warm. Somehow I had persuaded her to drive down the coast in a borrowed car for the afternoon, and she had brought an overnight bag. That was the day I fell in love with the world.

There was a fishing shack where an old woman cooked us lobsters for a dollar and sold us Carta Blanca beer for ten cents a bottle. When we were full and the sand was turning cool, she told us in Spanish how to find our way back to the village. Neither of us knew Spanish, but we followed the beach as she said, just a few feet ahead of the moon swept waves, until we heard music and found our hotel. Mornings then smelled like fresh sheets, and all our afternoons were full of sunshine. If Lillian were here, I would ask her why things are not like that now.

In the afternoons I sleep or go to crafts. I must sleep more often than I go to crafts, but I don't remember sleeping. I don't remember what I did in the afternoons before I came here. Don't people go to offices and sit at desks? I must have spent a long time doing something, but all those days have disappeared behind me like our wake on the ocean waves. Who can remember a single wave? Only here is life unchanging, like the time before birth or after death.

What I know now is sitting around a big table in our wheelchairs, staring at little piles of beads or colored papers. Crafts are a challenge for people with failing eyesight and nervous disorders. Only Mr. Jasper seems to enjoy them. As long as I have been here, he has been working on a model ship. At least it started out as a ship. He has glued airplane wings from another kit to the plastic hull, and waves it in the air in an imaginary dogfight. He will never finish it. Every day a few more pieces fall onto the floor, to be crunched into the carpet when they roll us back to our rooms "to freshen up" before dinner. No goddesses will call to him over the enchanted waves as we row past their island with covered ears.

Sometimes we go to the doctor. Going to the doctor is an adventure. They wheel us onto a special bus with a ramp that goes up and down. It is always a race to get to the medical arts building before someone has to go to the bathroom. If it happens in the bus, our caregivers have to clean it up; in the doctor's office, well, it's the nurses' problem. That's the rule, our caregivers say. The nurses don't always agree.

Then they roll us two or three at a time to the waiting room, where we sit around like we sit around outside the dining room waiting for our turn to eat. People in waiting rooms are not much fun. Like people in a restaurant ignored by their waiter, they scowl at newcomers, fearing someone else will be served first.

When Lillian was pregnant the first time, I went with her to all her doctor's appointments. Husbands were not allowed to see the doctor with their wives back then. She was so excited when she burst out after the examination, taking my hands and kissing me and saying, "Everything's fine!"

Nobody says, "Everything's fine" to me now. The doctor asks how I feel in a loud voice, so his nurse can write "no change" on my chart, and he can go on to another patient. That way they can get us back on the bus and out of there before somebody has another accident. Doctors were more attentive before they had alimony, second wives, children in college, and Mercedes-Benzes to worry about.

"I am having trouble sleeping," I replied.

The doctor and his nurse acted like I had slapped them. It may have been the first time I had spoken since, well, that may come to me someday, too.

"Did we start him on an antipsychotic last time?" the doctor asked the nurse.

"I don't think it's related to the medication," I continued. "It has something to do with a missing person."

"Who?" they asked together.

Her name, I think, is Lillian. Unlike the doctors and nurses when I was a boy, however, they could not hear my thoughts.

They looked at one another again, the nurse wrote something in my chart, and the doctor went on to the next patient. It is lonely sitting in those green rooms, wishing you were somewhere else but not sure where that would be. I am an oracle in a cave that no one enters.

When we ate at the club or a restaurant, she always let me choose the wine. The waiter would pour me a sip, and I would swirl it and smile over the glass at her before tasting. It was one of those games married people have played so long they forget how it started, but I remember. It was at the wedding, when the champagne bubbles went up her nose, and she laughed so hard everyone thought she had drunk the whole bottle.

"From now on, you go first," she cried and started laughing again.

We only had a weekend together, because the ship was sailing Monday morning. I still remember her on the pier in a light blue dress, pumps and white gloves, waving as happily as if I were leaving to go fishing with the children. That was another time, I think, but she always waved to us from the dock.

There is no wine list here. If you order ice tea, the ice is melted by the time you get it, and the lemon has sunk to the bottom. They serve bright colored vegetables, hard potatoes and chewy meat. It would be difficult to find the right wine for food like this.   On   the ship the food was much better, and you could see the bright blue ocean through the portholes. We were able to eat by ourselves, too, with white-coated stewards to serve us. If Mr. Jasper were here, he might remember. Perhaps they forgot to wake him up after lunch. Sometimes that happens to me.

When they finally remember to get you, all the food is gone, so they wheel you into the television room to get sleepy again. At night the people on TV yell at each other about somebody named Bush and what he and his friends are doing in Baghdad. Baghdad is the city where Aladdin flew on a magic carpe, and where Genghis Kahn built a mountain of human skulls outside the city gates. From the way people are insulting each other on television, I think there will be a mountain of skulls beside the city gates before anyone flies there again on a magic carpet.

Sometimes, when they leave me too long in front of the set, the screen goes blank and there is a fuzzy, rushing sound, as if thousands of insects were buzzing against the screen porch of our cabin at the lake. Then I change into an aerial sprite and hover close to the ceiling, where I can see the night nurse playing cards with the male orderly at the nursing station. If I stay near the ceiling, I can slip past them and creep silently through the dark rooms, looking for someone I recognize, someone who can still speak.

"Lillian?" I whispered, but it is not she.

My Lillian did not have an old woman's white hair and sleep with her mouth open. And here is Mr. Jasper, staring with yellow eyes at the ceiling. They should draw the blind at night; his face looks like wax in the moonlight. What could he be thinking that makes him forget to shut his eyes? If I had two coins, I would place them over his eyes, so that Charon would row him quickly away on his last voyage.

One of the others is awake.

"Are you Lillian?" I ask?

"Go away," she says, pulling the sheet up to her chin.

I must look like the angel of death, floating toward her bed. When the children were young, we took them out trick-or-treating on Halloween. When we came home, we all ate candy corn out of the bottoms of their sacks.

"Hey, Walt, man, you gotta go back to your room," the orderly says, taking my arm.

"We just started," I complain. "The next house has Hershey bars."

"Whoa," he says.

But it is too late. I, who navigated the ship across the wide Pacific, can surely find my way back to the sea. Oh, how I could run, if they had not wrapped me so tightly in plastic.

"That's cool, Walter, man," he says, setting me back in the wheelchair. "Let's get you some medicine so you can sleep."

I am too old for sleep. I want to be like Mr. Jasper; I want to die.

Why is he fastening the seat belt? Are we going to crash into the wall? Isn't Tiresias the one who can never die? What was magic draught I took that I should live forever?

The nurse serves me pills in a little paper cup, like a mother setting out candy at a birthday party. I always liked birthdays. Everyone here has forgotten how old they are, and they won't let us have sparklers. The pills are bitter, especially the green ones. That means they are very powerful.

The days now pass quickly, like waking moments in dreams. A middle-aged woman came to see me, but she could hardly speak. She just sat beside my bed, sobbing quietly. She looks like someone I might have known once.

Why has she ventured into the Sibyl's cave?

"Have you seen Lillian?" I finally asked to break the dismal spell.

"Oh, Daddy, you know she's gone."

Of course I know she's gone, but where? Outside? Is there still an outside? If I can find a tear in the screen, I will slip away and find her. But then what? Will one of the people in puffy blue gowns catch us in a net, dip us in chloroform and pin us in a glass case? No, I shall never go outside again.

The middle-aged woman showed me pictures of a young man in a black cap and gown. So they still have graduations. I wonder from what. Perhaps he is skilled in medicine, or law, or Slavic languages, or how to align the burial chamber in a pyramid with the North Star.

"You really must behave, Daddy. This is the last place in town we could find for you. Please don't cause any more trouble."

To show her how passive I am, I stop breathing. When I turn blue, she runs to the nursing station, and a large woman stalks in with an injection. I shall miss lunch again, I fear, but I do not miss company. My forays into society always end badly.

"Just try to be good, Daddy," she pleads. "Sometimes I think you have forgotten who you are."

She says that in the loud, self-righteous voice mothers use in supermarkets, when their children are running amuck. The large woman from the nursing station looks at her and nods. I am in for another afternoon alone in my room, with only the banging pipes for company. Like the blind seer, I do not speak because there is no one left to hear.

If you cannot see your own face, how can you know who you are? How can you be sure that you have not turned into someone else? Don't take mirrors for granted. I used to think there was one in the bathroom, but the last time I looked in it, the old man from the next room stared back at me. He hasn't had a haircut in a long time, and his face is lined and gray. His eyes have that shiny look that means he has forgotten who he is. I shall not look in there again.

Have I told you about Sundays? I know it is Sunday, because they wheel us into the TV room to watch Father Lawrence O'Grady, OFM say mass. I am not a Catholic, but that does not matter here. Father O'Grady carries out his sacred duties with the enthusiasm of a car salesman, who knows the people on the lot are just looking. Sometimes he doesn't turn off the TV. Perhaps he lacks self-confidence or doesn't want to miss a moment of "Meet the Press" or Robert Schuller's "Hour of Power."

After he leaves, just before bathroom time or lunch, Bishop L. Tyrone Washington of the New Canaan Church of God comes in with his band, and we really have some fun. They always turn off the TV, because they need the electrical outlet for their synthesizer. Oh, how I hate it if I have to go to the bathroom before lunch on Sunday. When the band plays, I can almost forget what I have lost. But when I turn to look at her and touch her hand, all I see are the pink, staring eyes of strangers, and oh, how quickly the music is over.

In his sermon Bishop Washington says that God is love. If I have known love, then I have known God. So finding Lillian has become my quest for the Holy Grail, my personal search for God. If she existed, then so does He. What does it matter if, as the middle-aged woman said, she isn't here any more? How long has it been since you saw God?

"Amen, Amen," I say, while the Bishop and his acolytes unplug the synthesizer and pack up their instruments.

As long as they are here, my caregiver is very patient.

"Good bye, Walter," the Bishop says, pressing my arm on the way out.

His fingers are so soft and warm.

"See you next time, man."

"Amen."

If Lillian were here, I would not be sitting around waiting for the Bishop to return. But she is not here. She is not anywhere anymore. So all I have is her memory and proof of the existence of God.

THE FORGIVENESS
OF EDWIN WATKINS

Two nights before he died, Edwin Watkins dreamed of a human heart. He had walked a great distance in a half-lit city carrying a cake box. Suddenly he was downtown in the elevator of the federal building, then at the huge conference table in his chambers with the white box before him. Behind him in the darkness, people were moving, but he did not know who they were. Suddenly he was afraid they knew what was in the box. He reached out to hide it, but the lid came off. Inside was a yellowish-gray heart with the aortas neatly cut, as if a pathologist had recently removed it from a cadaver.

Judge Watkins awoke sweating, as he often did when indigestion troubled him. He thought he had been asleep a long time, but the clock radio said it was only a little after eleven. Ellen, his wife, was still watching the news in the family room. He swung his legs over the side of the bed and sat breathing deeply until the heaviness in his chest subsided. When Ellen finally came upstairs, she knew he was pretending to be asleep. Her husband had pretended to be asleep when she came to bed for the last fifteen years.

Edwin Watkins became a lawyer, and then a judge, to act out the moral certainty pummeled into him by the priests and brothers at the orphanage where he was raised. One afternoon when he was seven, his parents drove away to the company picnic. Two days later he saw them again side-by-side in matching mahogany coffins placed beneath a larger than life crucifix bright with painted blood. Learning too early that to love is to endure almost unbearable pain, he retreated into the abstractions of the law with its mock precision and too real penalties.

The work ethic of the orphanage drove him to a successful career; civic duty demanded that he enter politics; rectitude required that he marry and father children. At fifty-two, the year his youngest finished college, he was appointed a federal district judge. With life time tenure assured by the United States Constitution, Edwin Watkins completed the division of humanity into the judges and the judged. Until his dream, he was supremely confident who occupied the judgment seat.

Judge Watkins had always enjoyed the day before a criminal docket. Assistant United States Attorneys and probation officers streamed into his chambers, solemnly submitting presentence investigations and recommendations against mercy. After their departure, he would read letters and pleas from the defendants' families and friends, explaining that the crime was a mistake or an aberration. The next day he might tell the letter writers that their affection for the defendant was misplaced, at least for the maximum term of incarceration. Many times he said nothing, watching the agony spread through his courtroom with grim satisfaction, like Jehovah numbering the afflictions of the Israelites. This day, however, Judge Watkins took no pleasure in the sins of his unwilling communicants. The U.S. Attorneys noticed he was staring at his pad without making notes, as he did before his legendary explosions. They glanced nervously at Linda Strickland, the Judge's law clerk, hoping she could explain his detachment in the ancient sign language of sycophants.

In her early thirties, unmarried, Ms. Strickland usually enjoyed the attention of the tense young men, who looked to her for some sign of the Judge's favor. Following his example, however, his clerk looked intently at her empty legal pad.

"What do you know about the human heart?" the Judge asked her as soon as their unhappy suitors had departed. .

Like many judges past middle age, he preferred the quieter company of female law clerks, whose reticence implied a sympathy unknown to their male counterparts. Looking at her deep brown eyes and teased blond hair, he realized she was the only woman he had been able to talk to since his youngest daughter left for college.

"Whose heart are we talking about, Judge?" Ms. Strickland answered brightly.

Had she not been as fascinated by Judge Watkins' courtroom tantrums as by his sometimes discerning intellect, she might have understood that it was her proximity to him that made her unapproachable to other men.

The judge looked at her with an expression of fear and wonder she had never seen before.

"Is that the right question?" he asked.

For several minutes, they both were silent.

"Tomorrow's docket," she finally said, without knowing how to finish the sentence.

"Five arraignments and one parole violation," he retorted, as if to demonstrate his attention to the morning's business. "Do you think it's one of theirs?"

"One of their whats?" Ms. Strickland inquired, fearing the answer.

"Their hearts."

"I don't know," replied Linda Strickland, reaching for her tablet. "Perhaps we'll find out tomorrow."

On the twenty-fifth floor of a building named for a burgeoning interstate bank, Harris Scintilton hurried from his office to peer through the glass doors into the reception area. An associate in the law firm of Tenninger, Waylind & Tour, the tweed-clad young man with round glasses and aristocratic features handled all the cases for indigent people that the federal court assigned to the firm.

"It's great experience," promised Douglas Frazier, head of the litigation department, in the same tone that recruiting officers once promised great experiences in the rice paddies of Vietnam.

Debonair, silver haired and consummately arrogant, Frazier relished the irony of assigning criminal cases to the firm's newest estate planner.

The young lawyer quickly learned that the experience was not to be shared with others, particularly the septuagenarian estate planning clients who sometimes gathered in the reception area, chirping happily in anticipation of cutting another relative out of their wills. Today Harris had to intercept La Ron Washington, charged with probation violation, before she collided with Mrs. Cuttleworth Ames coming to confer with Mr. Frazier about the outrageous claims of the Internal Revenue Service and a litigious passel of relatives disinherited by her late husband.

"You weren't going to meet with us, were you, Harris?" asked Mr. Frazier with silver toned condescension in the reception area.

Before the younger man could reply, the elevator doors opened, and La Ron Washington, elegant in hip-high black vinyl boots, a rabbit jacket and the remains of a mini skirt stepped out a pace ahead of Mrs. Ames. Equally elegant in her own fashion, the dowager Ames was clad in a floor length black mink coat that suffused the soft glow of unrestrained wealth and expensive perfume. Ms. Washington exuded musk and semen, and the bitter, evil smell of crack cocaine.

"For God's sake, get her out of here, " Frazier hissed to his associate, stepping forward to hurry Mrs. Ames down the parquet corridor, soft with Persian carpets, to the recesses of his corner office.

La Ron removed her sunglasses, which had frosted up in the elevator, and wiped them on a silver rayon blouse that extruded from her stole. Her orange-blond wig was slightly askew, contributing to her dishabille.

"Our situation is difficult," Harris began, closing the door to his office and retreating behind the desk.

Ms. Washington extracted a filter cigarette and a Bic lighter from an unlikely part of her couture. Encouraged by her attention, the young lawyer recounted how Judge Watkins had suspended her sentence when she was convicted for passing bad checks a year and a half earlier. Probation had been based on her promise to get a regular job, abstain from alcohol and drugs, and avoid her former associates. Harris was starting to read the particulars of the charge when she sniffed.

"Is something wrong?" he asked.

La Ron Washington stabbed her cigarette into his desk top ashtray and looked out the window.

"They say here you were arrested for theft and served six months in the state reformatory," he began again. As if to prolong her agony, the federal· bureaucracy had waited until she was released before charging her. "Your drug tests were positive, and . . ."

"An' the man I workin' fo' kick me out when I too pregnant to work the streets, and when I have the baby, he so small and weak . . ."

She started to cry. The lawyer didn't know what to do.

"Would you like a glass of water?" he asked.

Her face was buried in her hands, her sunglasses were on the floor, and she was sobbing uncontrollably.

"The baby die, Mr. Scintilton. They give 'im to me in the refo'matory, so I can see 'im die."

Tears transformed her from a caricature of crime to a human being in almost unspeakable agony. Harris lifted his phone to call his secretary, replaced it, and stepped around the desk to sit beside his client.

"Here," he said, handing her the tissues he kept for probate clients mourning more prosperous decedents. "We'll get through it somehow."

"What the judge gonna do to me now?" she said.

The only thing the law permitted Judge Watkins to do was impose the five-year sentence he had suspended when he placed her on probation. If he told her that, Harris' knew she would be dead before the case was called the next day. For the first time, Harris Scintilton had the experience of lying to a client. Instead of telling

La Ron that Judge Watkins would send her to the federal penitentiary, he told her that nobody ever knew what a judge would do.

"They say he tough," she said questioningly.

"Maybe he still has a heart," Harris replied.

La Ron smiled, wiped her face again, and let her lawyer guide her back to the elevators fifteen minutes before Mrs. Ames was scheduled to depart.

That night, the judge was sitting on the edge of the bed when Ellen came upstairs.

"Is anything the matter?" she asked, surprised he was not feigning sleep.

"My stomach," he replied. "I feel so full."

She sat down beside him and touched his forehead.

"You're not warm. I was afraid it was that flu everyone has."

He seemed relieved by her diagnosis.

"Just get a good night's sleep," she continued, patting his hand.

They both realized she was treating him like one of their children. She let go of his hand and stood up. He watched her go to the walk in closet to undress. In nearly forty years, neither of them had asked her to be anything more than a manikin. Suddenly it was very important to him that he return her touch.

"Ellen, I had the strangest dream last night," he began, breaking four decades of silence. "Do you know what it means to dream about a heart?"

"Where was it?" she asked from the closet, as if they often spoke of dreams before retiring.

"In a white cake box."

"A cake box?" she laughed. "Why would anyone carry their heart around in a cake box?"

He lay back in the bed and watched her turn off the light on the bedside table. When she laughed, she was almost girlish again. After she got into bed, he kissed her good night for the first time in fifteen years.

"What was that for?" she exclaimed.

"You've helped me with something that's been bothering me."

"The dream? How?"

"I finally have the right question."

Holding her arm, he closed his eyes, as if a great burden had been lifted from him. Ellen watched him fall quickly into a deep, dreamless sleep. The next morning he felt as if he had never gone to bed. No longer embarrassed by the intimacy a common bed implied, he touched her shoulder before leaving the house, and said he might come home early.

Whenever there was a criminal docket, Judge Watkins' dark paneled courtroom looked like an antechamber to hell. Before his huge raised bench, U.S. Attorneys filled the table nearest the jury box, and government agents and probation officers gathered at the other. In the shadow of the bench beside the witness chair sat the court reporter with newly dyed hair, stretching her long nylon legs, as bright as a fly among dung beetles.

Behind the brass bar that divided the courtroom, the handcuffed prisoners hunched in the first row. Lawyers with still free clients sat behind them, while family, friends and victims twisted on the other hard benches, or clustered helplessly along the walls. The door opened and shut constantly as lawyers looked for clients, the media and the misdirected sought the right courtroom, and a stream of high school students entered and left repeatedly in a search for civic understanding and public facilities. From the high walls larger than life portraits of Judge Watkins' black robed predecessors looked down, as insensately as from the bench on their own long forgotten cases.

Into this collision of statutory righteousness and human imperfection slipped Harris Scintilton, followed closely by La Ron Washington. The young attorney wore his dark blue three-piece suit; the client wore the same outfit that had sent tremors through Tenninger, Waylind & Tour, except she had traded her wig and sunglasses for a hamburger the night before. Her short, straightened hair was brushed back and down, making her appear younger and more afraid. They were squeezing into the back row when Linda Strickland stepped into the courtroom from the Judge's chambers and took up the gavel from her table.

No trumpeter for the mighty or diagnostician for the dying is watched as closely as a federal judge's clerk on sentencing day. The quiver of an eyelid meant the inevitable; a half smile bespoke hope. The courtroom was silent. Ms Strickland bent her head slightly, the watchers held their breath; soon the Honorable Edwin Watkins in death's black robe would enter with an executioner's quick pace and ascend the bench.

Edwin Watkins did not enter. After thirty seconds, the courtroom expired as one. There were whispers, then spoken questions. Where was the judge? Harris glanced at Ms. Washington. Her fists were clenched so tightly her hands quivered.

In the lavatory in his chambers, Judge Watkins' hands shook also as he braced himself at the sink, vomiting. When he finally looked up, he saw not the magnificent silver hair accentuating the stern expression, but blinking pink eyes staring out of sunken, bloodless flesh.

"They're waiting," he thought. Wetting a brown paper towel, he dabbed at his face. "I'll go home after the docket," he said to himself. "Ellen will know what to do."

When he finally opened the door to the courtroom, it was not Judge Watkins who bounded out to decry the failures of others, but a tired old man, sweating through his loose black robe.

The docket proceeded slowly. Three of the arraignments were lengthened when the accused withdrew their pleas of not guilty. In an incantation as invariable as a shaman's, Judge Watkins advised them of the rights they were foregoing in exchange for a quick exit from the purgatory of legal uncertainty, or the hope of a lighter sentence. At the back of the courtroom, Harris Scintilton looked at his watch and thought about all the billable hours he was losing. The most junior of the defense attorneys, his case was the last on the docket. His client, however, leaned forward, fascinated by the ritual.

Suddenly she pulled her lawyer's sleeve.

"He not so bad," she said. "He talk like he really care."

To Harris and the other lawyers, however, Judge Watkins' measured speech was the precursor to his rages that could destroy in moments a case or reputation built over years. At the conclusion of each case, the attorneys, agents and accused returned to their seats quickly, relieved the court's wrath had passed them by. When the case of United States of America versus La Ron Washington was finally called, everyone in the courtroom except Ms. Washington knew that the young attorney from Tenninger, Waylind & Tour would be on the receiving end. Eyes on the floor, she followed Scintilton through

the line of marshals, past the tables of government lawyers
and agents, like a sleeper in a nightmare of nakedness.

The Assistant U.S. Attorney read the charge, and
Harris replied that his client admitted the violation. Judge
Watkins was not listening to them; he was watching the
lines of type on the probation report bend and slide across
the page like lines of ice skaters.

"Your honor," the U.S. Attorney repeated. "Would
the court like a recitation of the facts?"

"Yes," the Judge replied automatically, returning
to the people before him. Suddenly the two young men in
three piece suits and the woman in the rabbit skin jacket
were as odd and interesting as the weaving letters.

"Probation Officer Jack Sherwood will state
the facts," announced the U.S. Attorney, turning to an
overweight man in his mid-fifties struggling to rise from
the agents' table.

"No," Judge Watkins snapped, himself for one last
moment. "I would like to hear the defendant's statement
of the facts."

Trembling, La Ron Washington raised her right
hand and, for the first time in her life, meant it when
she swore to tell the truth. Straight ahead was the court
reporter, acrylic nails poised over her stenotype machine.
Lifting her eyes and her voice at the same time, she began
to tell Edwin Watkins what had happened to her since she
last left his courtroom.

Death, drugs, depravity, and despair seldom had an
advocate like La Ron Washington. Voice steadily gaining
strength, she told the gray eyed old man above her about her
life as a prostitute, destitution when she was too pregnant
to work the streets, imprisonment for theft, and the awful
agony of her infant's death. As he looked down upon her,
then out at the silent, horrified courtroom, Judge Watkins

remembered the Masses in the orphanage, when he sat as terrified as the accused before the upraised Host.

Almost too late, he understood that all the law could do was command obedience and punish offense; it could never reconcile the penitent, forgive the sinner, or raise the dead. Before La Ron Washington, the law was as powerless as he himself would be before God. People were starting to fidget; the accused had finished her statement.

"Do counsel have anything to add," the Judge whispered.

"No, your honor," Harris and the U.S. attorney answered together, waiting for the explosion.

For the last time, Edwin Watkins drew himself up in his high back leather chair in the stern likeness of a federal judge.

"Can anyone here," he began, "tell me what threat this poor woman presents to the United States of America?"

Though the courtroom was filled with United States Attorneys, probation officers, and FBI agents, no one replied.

"Can anyone here tell me what good it will do to punish her, again and again?"

In that silence, Edwin Watkins finally stepped beyond judgment.

"Can anyone tell me anything she has not already suffered?"

Only the silence of the damned echoed him.

"Miss Washington," he said passionately, tears filling his eyes. "I will not violate your probation. This court will never violate your probation. The charges are dismissed. All of them. Dismissed!"

The men at the government tables before the bar were staring at the floor; behind the bar the handcuffed prisoners looked at each other in awe, amazed the universe still held hope.

"Is there anything else to come before this court?" Judge Watkins demanded.

Hearing nothing he arose, so dizzy he could hardly stand. The gavel banged from far away, and Ms. Strickland cried out the adjournment. Leaning against the wall, he lurched from the bench to his chambers. Something from a Mass at the orphanage had returned, and he had to write it down.

Behind him the government men grouped together, shaking their heads and marveling at Scintilton's unprecedented success. Quickly the people at the back who were still free crowded into the corridor, happy to escape. Harris said goodbye to his client at the elevator, where she was met by a young black man in white trousers and a black leather coat. She was wearing sunglasses again, but he knew she was looking at him proudly.

"Did you hear what happened to Ed Watkins?" Mr. Frazier cried from the door to Harris' office.

The associate had worked late to make up for the time lost in court, and had not seen the newspaper the next morning.

"Died of a heart attack in his chambers," Frazier continued. "I hope he got your entry on before it happened."

Like most litigators Douglas Frazier was always vaguely displeased by another lawyer's courtroom success.

"I'll check," Harris said nervously.

If the order not violating Ms. Washington's probation were not signed before the Judge's death, it would not be effective.

Linda Strickland met Harris in the waiting room, and led him into chambers. Blue case folders were neatly stacked along one side of the long conference table. At the end where the judge sat, .the chair was pushed back, as if he had just left for a moment. One crumpled paper lay on his workspace.

"I called the other lawyers from yesterday's docket," she said, when he explained his errand. "There's nothing to worry about. He always wrote out his own entries right after court."

Her voice broke; Edwin Watkins' death meant more to her than an imperiled courtroom victory.

"I'm sorry, Linda," Scintilton said, wondering why she had not called him.

"You don't have to say that," she said bitterly. "None of the others were sorry."

For a federal judge, death meant a solemn convocation of the surviving judges to read stilted tributes, a memorial photograph in a hard back law book, and a medley of calls to senators from would be successors.

She picked up the paper from the judge's workspace, and handed it to the lawyer. The case caption was typed at the top. In oversize letters, Edwin Watkins had printed his last order: "Denied. This Court will never violate Defendant's probation. WATKINS, J." Underneath something was written in a cramped script that ended in a smear.

"Do you recognize it?" Linda asked.

"'The law was given through Moses, but . . . '" Harris read.

The Judge's heart had stopped before he finished the sentence.

"What does it mean?" she wondered.

"'But truth and grace came through Jesus Christ,'" Harris said. "It's from the first chapter of Saint John's Gospel."

Ms. Strickland sat down in Judge Watkins' chair and covered her eyes with her hands.

"He called me just before it happened," she sobbed. "He said to come in right away. He had remembered something very important. But when I came in . . ."

"He had a big heart," said Harris Scintilton, touching her shoulder.

She looked at him in wonder, as if a great mystery had been revealed.

"It was his heart," she said. "He never lost it."

Harris was still holding the paper.

"Are you going to be alright?" he asked, amazed at the change in her.

She nodded.

"I'd like a copy sometime."

"They'll give you the original at the clerk of court's office after it's entered," she explained, the law clerk once again.

Harris framed the order and placed it on the inside of the credenza beside his phone, where only he could see it. When opposing counsel made unreasonable demands, or clients rejected his advice, or a case went against him, he would remember La Ron Washington, Edwin Watkins, and the strange acts of grace that sometimes proceeded from the dying and from the mouth of God.

THE ANNUNCIATION
OF CHARLES SPEARS

"Your Angel stinks," said Timmy Ames and flapped off in his shepherd's costume.

The Reverend Charles Spears, Rector of the Downtown Church of Our Savior, thought he had seen his last Christmas pageant. The average age of his parishioners was seventy-three, and he had not had a christening in years. Then Dorothy Ames, Timmy's grandmother, suggested that the grandchildren put on the play.

"It won't work, Dorothy," he tried to dissuade her. "Grandparents can't control their grandchildren. That's the secret of the relationship."

The dowager empress of the Ames Machinery Company was not to be thwarted; the church's budget and Spears' salary depended on her munificence. Soon all the grandmothers were arguing over whose grandchild would have the speaking parts as Mary, the Innkeeper, or the Angel Gabriel. Spears finally had to assign the parts by lot to keep the parish from splitting into factions.

Now, as one grandmother after another realized that she didn't have the strength to control a howling three year old, and the children quarreled and sulked and wailed, the Rector had to deal with a drunk. Entering the nave, he recognized the hunched shoulders silhouetted against the brightly-lit manger before the altar. Timmy's angel was a refugee from the Alcoholic Drop In Center, who came to the church for handouts after drinking up his disability compensation. The priest was wondering where he could ask him to sit to avoid offending the suburban sensibilities of his parish, when Mrs. Ames rushed down the aisle.

"Melissa's children are sick," she cried. "We don't have any angels."

"Maybe I could help out," the drunk in the filthy black raincoat said from the first pew.

Timmy's angel had a deeply lined face, yellow teeth and compelling brown eyes, framed by long greasy hair and a heavy gray beard. Dorothy Ames stared at him, caught her breath and gagged. He reeked of tobacco, perspiration and back alley wine. The dowager Ames stalked away.

"Was it something I said?" asked the Angel.

His shoulders twitched under his coat like a dog rubbing its hind legs together.

"Just, well, the children," the Rector said, afraid the Angel had the DTs.

"Don't worry, Bud," the Angel replied thickly. "I'll take care nobody messes up their lines."

Stooped, graying, Charles Spears had that tired, strained, tormented look that Episcopalians value in their clergy. Unable to decide anything, he remained a bachelor at sixty-four, attractive to his septuagenarian female parishioners in the same helpless way as their hairdressers and their pets. Soon, however, the Rector would have to decide whether to accept the anonymous poverty administered by the Church Pension Fund or to continue a ministry in which even he had lost faith.

So Charles Spears walked away from he Angel just as he had walked away from every other problem in his life and went to the vesting room to prepare for the service. When he returned the narthex was crowded with acolytes, choir members, and elderly women trying to herd their manic grandchildren into line. If I take it just one minute at a time, Spears thought, I can get through this. By seven o'clock I'll be opening a bottle of cabernet and thanking God it's all over for another year.

Then the organ sounded the first chords of "O Come, All Ye Faithful," the acolytes raised their candles and crosses, and the procession started down the aisle. Following the choir was the cast for the Christmas pageant in the final throes of stage fright and excitement, twisting their hands away from their frantic grandmothers. The last thing that Spears heard before entering the nave was Dorothy Ames calling, "Don't you understand? There aren't any angels."

Spears was on automatic pilot through the opening prayers. Now all he had to do was sit, smile, and hope nobody forgot their lines. Right on cue, a nine-year-old Ames granddaughter mounted the lectern and began to read the Christmas story from the Gospel according to Luke.

"And in the sixth month the angel Gabriel was sent from God unto a city in Galilee, named Nazareth, to a virgin espoused to a man whose name was Joseph, of the house of David; and the virgin's name was Mary."

Spears blinked as a spotlight illuminated a five-year old miniature Mary clothed like a Carmelite nun in blue habit and white cowl.

"And the angel came in to her and said . . ."

Time stopped. In the side aisle Dorothy Ames threw up her hands and grimaced; there was no angel. Spears was turning to signal the choir director to start the "Magnificat" when he heard something like a rug being shaken out, and a smell like wet dog enveloped him. He looked down into the nave. The Angel had caught his raincoat on his wings and was flapping them to shake it loose. Mary pointed where it was stuck, and the Angel yanked it free and dropped it on the pew. Then he knelt before the amazed virgin. Heavy with dirty white feathers, his wings shuddered in the spotlight.

"Hail thou that art highly favored, the Lord is with thee," he coughed in a voice rough with tobacco and phlegm.

He was wearing green and orange plaid bellbottoms, oversize gym shoes and a yellow T shirt that said "American College of Obstetricians and Gynecologists – Tampa 1999."

"Blessed art thou among women," he continued, and the ancient lines caught fire.

Clapping her hands, Mary jumped up and down and giggled. When it was time for her to question the heavenly messenger, the Angel had to whisper her lines and have her repeat after him. Mary was quiet as the Angel announced the miracle that was to be.

Another great silence. Who, Spears wondered, could speak in the presence of angels?

Mary reached out to touch the Angel's beard.

"Behold the handmaid of the Lord," she said. "Be it unto me according to thy word."

The Angel stood up, made a low sweeping bow, and spread his wings. Like a tired fisherman rowing back to shore, he pulled himself into the air. The rest of the cast rushed forward as he was heaving himself toward the vaulted ceiling. Timmy Ames jumped up and touched the Angel's shoe before his Grandmother could yank him back.

"Go wash your hands," she snapped.

But he twisted away, and the show went on.

"And Mary arose in those days, and went into the hill country with haste, into a city of Judah, and entered into the house of Zacharias, and saluted Elizabeth."

The narrator stopped while Mrs. Ames sorted through the cast until she found Elizabeth. Just one more line, Spears thought, and the choir will sing the Magnificat, and the pageant will be half over.

"Say something," Mrs. Ames said to the terrified Elizabeth.

The little girl looked up at the Angel, who was sitting on the crossbeam over the altar, panting. The Angel cupped his hands and mouthed the next line.

"Blessed art thou among women, and blessed is the fruit of thy womb."

Behind him, Spears heard the choir standing up. They would steal Mary's best lines, and a brilliant cantata would once again overwhelm the Incarnation.

"My soul doth magnify the Lord," a countertenor sounded from the rafters.

Before the director could bring down the baton, Mary answered, "And my spirit hath rejoiced in God my Savior."

Then their voices blended in a wild, atonal wail as they shared the exaltation of Mary, the downfall of the mighty, and the coming salvation of Israel. Robes whooshing like deflated balloons, the choir sat down, and the director cringed at chords that had not been heard since Pharaoh's chariots capsized in the onrushing sea. This was not Christmas music; this was the paean of the daughters of Israel as they stripped the bodies of the drowned Egyptians. Then silence, the silence of the stopped heart, while parents and grandparents stared at the frozen actors, terrified that Herod's soldiers would appear to carry off the Holy Innocents.

"And it came to pass in those days, that there went out a decree from Caesar Augustus, that all the world should be taxed," the narrator read, and the drama continued.

Joseph appeared with a cardboard donkey and walked around the altar with Mary to signify the long winter journey from Nazareth to Bethlehem. Rejected by the Innkeeper, they sat down in the manger before a crib. As the shepherds emerged from the side aisle, Mary accomplished the miraculous birth by lifting the covers from a doll in the crib. Timmy Ames grabbed one of the plastic sheep from the manger and stepped back into the star lit field.

For the first time in the history of Christmas pageants, when the Angel appeared, there was real fear. Sliding off the crossbeam he lost his grip and bumped his left wing. The cast scattered as he tumbled down in a slow motion cartwheel and landed hard on the communion rail.

"Damn," he muttered under his breath. "That hurt."

"You're supposed to say, 'Fear not,'" the narrator prompted him.

Stubbed wing shuddering, the Angel stood up on the rail.

"Fear not," he said in a voice so warm and reassuring that even Timmy Ames' father, who had just been cited for driving under the influence for the second time that holiday season, relaxed. "For unto you is born this day in the city of David a Savior, which is Christ the Lord."

It was the Angel's big moment, when he was joined with a multitude of the heavenly host. But there wasn't any heavenly host; there were just two shepherds and the Three Wise Men waiting in the aisle.

"Let's try something," the Angel said to the shepherds.

Taking Timmy in his right hand and the other shepherd in his left, he lifted off the floor like a ballet dancer, wings barely moving. They rose with the spotlight to the highest point in the cathedral ceiling where he released the two boys. For a second they hovered beside him, waving at their friends while their grandmothers covered their mouths in horror. Then they lost their balance and wobbled back down like kids on their first two wheelers. The Angel sank onto the crossbeam and signaled the narrator to move on to the Wise Men. The spotlight returned to earth, and the Angel faded into the darkness like Giotto's angels in Santa Croce when the coin operated lights go out.

The rest of the service was almost ordinary. Reclaiming its place, the choir sang Stanford's Magnificat in C during the offertory. Spears smelled the Angel before he saw him at the communion rail and pressed the wafer into his tobacco stained fingers. He had put on his raincoat again, and as the priest moved on to the next communicant, he heard him slurping the communion wine.

The choir director wouldn't even look at Spears after the service. Most of the grandmothers stalked out with their charges without speaking, and the other parishioners reacted as they had to his one attempt to use the contemporary version of the Lord's Prayer.

"Nice to do something different once in a while, Charles," they said. "But not as a steady diet."

The only one who looked like she had enjoyed it was Mary, who wiggled her fingers at Spears as her father carried her outside to the car. The Angel was the last to emerge from the nave.

"Quite a team, weren't we, Bud?" he cried.

The Rector held his breath and turned away, only to see Mrs. Ames stalking toward him dragging Timmy by the hand.

"I don't know what you were thinking about with these children, Charles," she began before turning on the Angel. "And that was the worst Magnificat I ever heard!"

"Guess you had to be there, lady," the Angel replied.

"Where did you learn to fly?" Timmy asked.

"We'll talk about that some day, son," the Angel said.

"And we will, too, Charles!" Mrs. Ames snapped, leading her reluctant shepherd away.

"Got anything to drink?" asked the Angel.

"Come on," the Rector said leading him to the elevator to his apartment in the tower.

Spears always looked forward to Christmas Eve, when he could be alone with his wine and his memories. He had set aside enough food from the parish Christmas supper to last the weekend, and had a bottle of cabernet waiting for him on the credenza in the tiny dining room. When he opened the door, the Angel followed him to the kitchen and took off his coat. He watched the priest take the roast beef and potatoes out of the refrigerator and put them in the microwave.

"Would you like a salad?" Spears asked.

"Can't tell you how long it's been since I had a salad," the Angel answered.

"Why don't you go into the dining room and open the wine," Spears said, handing him the glasses.

As soon as he was gone, the priest cracked the window and took a deep breath. He heard the cork pop in the next room.

"Ah," exclaimed the Angel.

When the priest carried in the plates, the Angel was holding a glass under his nose, inhaling deeply.

"This isn't the kind that gets you into the Drop In Center," he said.

"What's it like living there?" Spears wondered.

The Angel looked at him expectantly. The priest said a quick blessing. Then the Angel drank deeply and started on his dinner.

"Trouble with the Center is I have to wait until everybody's asleep to shower up," he said between mouthfuls. "Last time a guy saw these wings, they put him in the state hospital for six months."

The Angel refilled his glass.

"God, this is good stuff, Bud."

"Why do you drink so much?" the priest asked.

"Probably the same reason you do," the Angel replied. "You're part of something big once, and you think everything's going to change. But it doesn't, and you can't understand why. You know it really happened because you were there, but the years keep rolling on by."

"Like being ordained," Spears said softly.

"There you go," said the Angel. "Or being in the Army. Or for the women, maybe like having a baby. You keep thinking something wonderful will happen again, maybe to somebody else, you'd settle for that, but it's totally out of your control. So I've been waiting and remembering all this time and still nothing happens. I guess that's why I drink."

"I've got some mince pie," Spears suggested.

"That would be great."

Spears went to the kitchen for the pie and stood by the window, inhaling the cold air while the coffee brewed. When he returned with dessert and coffee, the Angel was finishing the wine in the priest's glass.

"Glad we got a chance to talk, Bud," the Angel said.

"So am I."

The Angel followed him into the kitchen with his dishes and looked at the open window. Outside streetlights stretched across the downtown basin toward the hills that surrounded the city. Only a few cars moved along the snow dusted streets. The night was silent.

"I better be going now, Bud," the Angel said. "They lock up the Center at ten o'clock."

They shook hands. To Spears' surprise, the Angel's hand was soft, as if he had never worked. The Angel picked up his raincoat.

"I'll let myself out," he said.

He opened the window all the way and climbed up onto the sill. Then he stepped out into the starry night.

ACKNOWLEDGMENTS

The Butterfly Collector - *Toyon* 2004 (Winner of Raymond Carver Contest at Humboldt State University)

The Beautician - *Dreams and Visions* No. 33 (2004)

Two Cures for Phantom Limb - *Raconteur* Vol. 3, No. 1 August 1995

Breaking Cover - *Gray's Sporting Journal* Vol. 28 No. 4 August 2003

Not Until Everything's Perfect - *Rosebud* Issue 18 (Fall 2000)

The Resurrection of Nelson Campbell - *The Adirondack Review* (Fall 2009)

A Gracious Voice - *Short Story International* Vol. 113 (1996)

The Historian - *Takahe 60* (April 2007)

Embracing the Inner Child - *Pearl 38* (December 2007)

The Deer - *Storyglossia.com* Issue 30 (October 2008)

A Friend of Bill Gillen - *Pearl 36* (December 2006)

Lillian - *Storyglossia.com* Issue 18(March 2007)

The Forgiveness of Edwin Watkins - *Dreams & Visions* No. 24 (Winter 1998)

FRED McGAVRAN was an English major at Kenyon College and served as an officer in the Navy in Vietnam. A graduate of Harvard Law School, he defends psychiatric malpractice claims and represents veterans in claims against the Veterans Administration as counsel for Frost Brown Todd LLC in Cincinnati, Ohio. He is a candidate for ordination as a deacon in the Episcopal Diocese of Southern Ohio.

McGavran won the 2007 *Writers Digest* Short Story Contest in the horror category, the 2004 John Reid/Tom Howard Contest, the 2003 Raymond Carver Award from Humboldt State University, and has placed in a number of other literary and screenwriting contests. His stories have appeared in *Pearl Magazine, Rosebud, Gray's Sporting Journal, Dreams & Visions, Storyglossia, Short Story International,* and other literary magazines and e-zines. The Ohio Arts Council awarded him a $10,000 Individual Achievement Award in 2009 for his story "The Reincarnation of Horlach Spenser." He won the 2008 St. Lawrence Prize for *The Butterfly Collector.* McGavran lives in Cincinnati with his wife Liz, a decorator. They have two daughters, Sarah, who is working on a PhD in art history at Washington University, and Marian, who is a paralegal in San Diego.